ÉCLAIR MURDER

A Patisserie Mystery Book 2

HARPER LIN

This is a work of fiction. Names, characters, organizations, places, events, and incidents are either products of the author's imagination or are used fictitiously. Some street names and locations in Paris are real, and others are fictitious.

ÉCLAIR MURDER Copyright © 2014 by Harper Lin.

ISBN-13: 978-0992027995

ISBN-10: 0992027993

www.harperlin.com

CHAPTER ONE

A month after returning to her hometown from her travels abroad, Clémence Damour was back into the swing of Parisian life without the tedious routine that came with living in the city. She knew she was lucky to avoid the *Métro, boulot, dodo,* the subway-work-sleep routine that was the unfortunate fate of other Parisians. Working eleven-hour days had never been her goal. What she did for a living she didn't even consider work but play.

Her family's patisserie chain, Damour, made some of France's most delicious desserts and pastries. Aside from the flagship store in the 16th arrondissement, there were two other locations in Paris that Clémence checked up on from time to time. Her parents were away in Asia for at least six months, and not only was she house-sitting and dog-sitting for them, but she got to take over in inventing new dessert flavors with the patisserie's head baker, Sebastien Soulier.

But by Thursday afternoon, she was feeling the fatigue. Because work was so much fun, she'd been spending seven days a week in the kitchen without even noticing it. She and Sebastien were experimenting with savory éclairs for the *salon de thé* lunch menu. Some of the results had been downright awful. She decided to leave work early and walk her dog Miffy at the park to relax and spend some time under the sun.

It was spring in Paris. The trees on the streets and boulevards were in bloom. As she walked down the steps of the Palais de Chaillot with Miffy, she passed by the lovely flowers in the gardens and the fresh green foliage of the trees and the dewy grass. The grand fountain was turned on, and kids squealed as they splashed their hands in the water. A few skateboarders did flips and tricks while the tourists on the viewing platform above took pictures of *la Tour Eiffel* in awe.

She was heading across the Seine to the Champs de Mars, the park beneath the tower. She passed the thick aroma of crêpe and waffle stands, where Miffy was compelled to linger. The sun was still three hours away from setting, so they had plenty of time to enjoy the blue clouds and the light of day. One never knew when the sun was going to appear in Paris, and when it did, everybody was out to take advantage of it.

Clémence walked around, looking for other dogs so that Miffy could socialize. She spotted a fluffy Pomeranian dog on the other side of the field and wondered if the lady holding the leash would mind if Miffy interacted with the dog a bit. She made her way toward them, passing teenagers taking selfies and vendors selling illegal keychains and trinkets in the shape of the original tower.

As they walked, they were accosted by a Jack Russell terrier with a red bandana tied around the neck.

Arthur Dubois, her neighbor, greeted her with a strained smile. He was as handsome as always, dressed in a white dress shirt and crisp blue jeans. His chestnut brown hair was neatly combed, and his brown eyes seemed to examine her with curiosity.

"*Bonjour*, Arthur," Clémence said with a polite smile. She still wasn't sure whether their greeting required bisous, kisses on the cheeks, since they were not particularly close.

"Bonjour," he replied stiffly.

They had been on the verge of some sort of friendship when Arthur had found her unconscious on the street last month and called for an ambulance when she had been investigating who had killed la gardienne, the caretaker of their building. Once in a while, she was able to discern a soft side from his snotty façade, but it was as rare to encounter as a French person who didn't like cheese.

The Russell terrier and Miffy were wagging their tails happily and jumping up and down. The dogs were pals, since Arthur's family had dog-sat Miffy before, and Clémence would've suggested walking the dogs together more often if Arthur wasn't so downright rude sometimes.

After Clémence helped Inspector Cyril St. Clair find the killer, she had received a big bouquet of beautiful pink and red roses that had been left in front of her apartment door. No note came with it to say whom the bouquet was from, but she suspected that it had been from Arthur. The last time she'd run into Arthur, she'd asked whether the roses were from him, but he had vehemently denied it.

"Why would I give you flowers?" he asked, a bit nastily.

Clémence immediately felt stupid for asking. He probably thought she was insinuating that he had romantic interest in her. His family had been victims in the whole debacle, and Clémence had uncovered the truth. Plus she had been beaten and almost killed in the process. Didn't that warrant flowers?

"Nobody in your family sent it either?" Clémence had asked.

"Not as far as I know," he replied.

If the Dubois family didn't send it, then who did? In any case, she didn't appreciate Arthur's attitude, and the whole exchange had made her apprehensive about him again.

But here he was with his dog. And he was walking next to her.

"Hey, what is your dog's name?" she asked.

"You mean after all these years, you never knew his name?"

Clémence fumed. She was trying to be polite, but he was making it difficult, as usual.

"I was away for two years," she said. "And this is maybe one of the few times I have seen your dog."

"It's Youki," he replied.

"Oh."

Clémence wanted their walk to be over, but Miffy was really enjoying herself with Youki. She had come to the park to socialize Miffy, after all.

"How's the PhD going?" she asked, to dispel the uncomfortable silence between them.

"Well," he said.

"What's it about, anyway?"

"Macroeconomics," he said. "But nothing you would understand because it's quite complicated."

Clémence silently called him a few names. Did he realize how rude he was being, or was it just a part of his personality?

She decided not to react, but she wouldn't make the effort to make any more conversation. As soon as Miffy received sufficient time with Youki, she would make her excuses and walk the other way.

After another bout of awkward silence, Arthur finally spoke up. "Any new macaron flavors at Damour?"

"Yes," Clémence said. "We've just launched a cherry blossom flavor, and—"

She was interrupted by Youki running off in the

park, toward two guys who were throwing a Frisbee around. Arthur must've had a loose grasp of the leash, and he chased after Youki.

Miffy wanted to go after them, too. She barked excitedly, but Clémence held the leash tight.

"Stay here, Miffy. I guess we'll wait for them."

After all, she couldn't just go home now. It was amusing to watch Arthur chasing after Youki and looking frazzled.

Clémence laughed as she watched them, but when she looked down at Miffy few minutes later, she realized that the dog had stretched the extended leash all the way to a bush.

"Miffy?"

Her dog was sniffing an éclair on the ground near the bush. Sticking out of the bush were shoes. Men's shiny brown shoes.

"What the…?"

Clémence pulled Miffy back and looked into the bush. The pants seemed to be made of expensive fabric, and the shoes were high-end as well; it couldn't have been a homeless man.

"Monsieur?" she called. "Are you okay?"

The man didn't answer.

Miffy was still sniffing the piece of éclair on the ground, but she wasn't licking it.

"Okay, Miffy, stop."

Clémence looked back at Arthur, who was walking toward them with Youki.

"I think this man needs help!" Clémence said to Arthur.

Arthur ran to them, and he parted the bush. The man lying in it was in his mid to late forties, with dark brown hair and tortoiseshell spectacles. He wore a business suit and tie, like a typical Parisian man working in the area.

Arthur checked for a pulse. He grimaced and stepped back.

"I think he's dead," Arthur said weakly.

CHAPTER TWO

"Dead?" Clémence croaked. She looked around the park incredulously, but nobody else was within earshot.

Arthur nodded, looking at his hand, which had just touched a dead man.

Clémence wasted no time in pulling out her phone and calling the police.

"How could this happen?" she wondered out loud. "There's no blood or anything. And in broad daylight?"

"I don't know, but let's step away."

They pulled their dogs to a nearby bench. Arthur sat, but Clémence couldn't help but remain standing. She strained her neck to look at the body.

"Come on," said Arthur. "You're drawing attention to it."

Clémence didn't listen. She pushed Miffy's leash into Arthur's hands and left before he could object. She found the courage to go back to the corpse in the bush.

Was the man really dead? And the éclair he'd been eating—it looked awfully like the one from her store. It was pistachio flavored, and Clémence recognized the exact shade of the green cream filling oozing out from the choux pastry.

She held her breath and parted the bush.

"What are you doing?" Arthur said, coming up behind her with the dogs. "You don't want to get involved in another murder, do you?"

Clémence noticed a lavender paper bag in the bush, close to the body. Just as she suspected. Lavender was Damour's brand color, and sure enough, the bag was imprinted with the store's gold logo.

"This man had been eating a pistachio éclair from my shop before he died," she said.

"Not so loud," Arthur said. "There are children walking by."

"I can't believe it," she said in a lowered voice. "This makes no sense. It must be a medical condition." Then she began to panic a little. "Oh God, what if he was allergic to something in the éclair? We use fresh ingredients. But what if it's our fault?"

"Calm down," said Arthur, even though he was worked up himself. "Will you just come back to the bench? Oh look—the police are here."

A police car pulled up, followed by the emergency response workers in a pompier truck.

Clémence told them what they had discovered, and the police quickly sectioned off their part of the park with police tape, telling picnickers to pack up and move.

Soon another car pulled up, a black smart car. Clémence was amused to see the lanky Inspector Cyril St. Clair getting out of the tiny car. Cyril was tall and green bean–thin, with gaunt cheeks, a hawk nose and sharp green eyes. He reminded her of a vulture.

"You again," he called. "Where there's murder, there's la heiress."

Clémence sighed. Did this fool of an inspector always have to be such a bully?

"Well, my dog seems to have a nose for finding dead bodies," she said wryly. "Maybe she should have an office of her own at 36 Quai des Orfèvres."

Arthur swallowed a laugh. This was certainly

not the moment to be comedic, Clémence knew, but if Cyril was going to be nasty and sarcastic, she would have a laugh too.

"Who is he?" Cyril nodded toward the dead body in the bush.

"Aucune idée," said Arthur. "No clue. We just found him in the bush when we were walking our dogs."

Cyril demanded that they tell him everything from the beginning. He took notes, then poked around the body like the rest of his team.

"He had been eating pistachio éclairs from Damour?" Cyril turned around, holding a plastic bag that contained the nub of the éclair. In his other hand was the lavender paper bag in another plastic bag.

Clémence shrugged. "Our pastries are very popular in this neighborhood. I don't know what happened."

Cyril narrowed his sharp eyes at her. "I knew your pastries were poison."

Clémence put a hand on her hip. "If you so much as suggest to the media that our products are poisonous, my parents will have their lawyers on you in an instant."

"We don't know what happened," Arthur said.

"So everybody just calm down. He could've just had some sort of medical condition, like epilepsy."

"And nobody noticed him fall into the bush?" Cyril asked.

"Are there any security cameras around the tower?" asked Clémence. "Maybe you can find out that way."

"Leave the investigating to me," said Cyril. "I'm the inspector, remember? Not some amateur baker."

Clémence bit her tongue, literally, to keep from lashing back at Cyril. Sure, she didn't go to baking school and she was the heiress to the most popular patisserie and tea salon chain in Paris, but she was no amateur baker. She had learned from the best— her parents—and she had graduated from one of the best art schools in the country. But she didn't want to say all that to Cyril, as she'd be wasting her breath.

"I did solve the last murder, remember?" she said as calmly as she could. "I never got a thank-you note for that."

"Well, I could've solved it if you and your dog hadn't ruined the investigation."

"Oh, please." Clémence rolled her eyes. "We—"

"Maybe we should go," said Arthur. "We'll leave you to your investigation, since we've already told you all we know. If you want to ask anything else, you know where to reach us."

He pulled Clémence away.

"I want to smack that guy every time I see him," Clémence said.

"Which is why I pulled you away." There was a hint of a smile on Arthur's face. "I don't want you to end up in jail for beating up an inspector."

Clémence took a few deep breaths. "Fine. You're right. I can't let him get to me."

They walked back toward the tower and then to their building. Clémence thought about taking a bath to relax. This was the second time in a month that she'd seen a dead body. At least it was a stranger this time.

"Just go home," Arthur said. "We don't even know if there is a killer. Like I said, the man could've died from natural causes."

"Killer?" Clémence hadn't even thought about another killer being involved until Arthur mentioned it. But it was entirely possible.

CHAPTER THREE

When Clémence went into work the next morning, she had nearly forgotten about the dead body in the bush. She hoped that this was the end of her spell of finding dead bodies in Paris. In the kitchen, she busied herself with testing Sebastien's savory éclairs. This one was stuffed with salmon, a mousse-like cream cheese, and fresh herbs.

"You've done it," she said. "This is going on the lunch menu."

Sebastien beamed. "Did you still want me to work on the hot dog éclair?"

The hot dog éclair was basically a wiener in the éclair's "choux" shell—a gourmet hot dog with a French twist.

Clémence nodded. "Yes. It doesn't taste quite right yet. I want the perfect balance of French and American. Right now, it's tasting too French."

Damour pastries often had an American or international twist. It was the fusion between the classic and the new that made the chain so popular.

"What is it about it that's so French?" Sebastien asked.

"It's the ketchup and mustard," said Clémence.

"But it's freshly made," Sebastien protested. "It's perfect."

"Yes, but American ketchup has more sugar."

Sebastien wrinkled his freckled nose. "You want me to add more sugar to this perfectly good home-made tomato ketchup? Why don't we just use a bottle of Heinz then!"

Sebastien was being sarcastic, but Clémence took this idea seriously. Her mother was American, and she'd lived in New York during many summers growing up. She knew how good a New York hot dog from a street vendor could be.

"Heinz…" she said. "Okay, let's try it. I think that's the only thing keeping that recipe from being a hit."

"You can't be serious," Sebastien muttered, but he called up one of the intern bakers to try to find some authentic American ketchup. The intern took a break from slicing vanilla beans in half for their vanilla macaron recipe to go to an American shop in the 7th arrondissement.

"In the meanwhile, let's work on the shrimp and avocado éclairs," Clémence said.

Berenice came back from her break with a strange look on her face. She was Sebastien's younger sister, and also a baker. Both Soulier siblings had reddish-brown hair and pale, freckled skin. Sebastien was more serious and secretive, while Berenice was a lot more spirited and chatty.

"Hey, Clémence," Berenice said. "There's a couple of police cars outside the patisserie. Caroline's talking to the police right now, and they're causing a commotion with the customers."

Caroline was Damour's head manager. Clémence wiped her hands on her apron. She was about to head out the door to see what was going on when Caroline came in with Inspector Cyril St. Clair.

Clémence groaned.

"The feeling is mutual, Mademoiselle Damour," Cyril said.

Caroline, who was usually calm and collected, had panic in her eyes. "He says we have to close down the entire place for the day. They want to inspect for poison."

"What?" Clémence exclaimed.

"Qu'est-ce qui se passe?" Sebastien asked. "What's going on?"

All the chefs and bakers in the kitchen turned to stare at Cyril and his men.

"A man was found dead this morning at the Champs de Mars," Cyril declared. "He died from eating poisoned éclairs from your patisserie."

"Poisoned?" Berenice said.

"Yes. That's right." Cyril paced the kitchen with his long spidery legs. "One and a half pistachio éclairs from Damour was enough to kill a healthy forty-three-year-old man. We are shutting down the entire shop to check for traces of poison."

"Tell me you did not announce this loud enough for the customers to hear," said Clémence.

"I pulled him to the back before he did," said Caroline.

Cyril rolled his eyes. "Did you hear what I said? I need everybody out. My team is going to check every nook and cranny for anything suspicious."

"But you can't do that," Clémence implored. "This is ridiculous. We're not lacing our pastries with poison. Our *salon* is full, and have you seen the lineup for the patisserie? We can't shut down now. You have nothing on us."

"It's for the good of the customers," Cyril insisted. "We can't have another one dropping dead from poison, can we now? Everybody out."

The employees looked at each other, then looked to Caroline and Clémence for further instruction.

"Fine," Clémence said. "Caroline, please come up with something and inform the customers that we'll be closed for the morning."

"Not just the morning." Cyril smiled slyly. "We might need the entire day. Maybe even tomorrow."

"That's just not right." Heat rose to Clémence's cheeks. "First of all, you're wasting your time. And you're not only wasting our time, but our business, as well."

"I'm so sorry that you'll be losing a few dollars," said Cyril, "but I think a police investigation is more important than selling a few macarons, don't you think?"

"We have lunch reservations to fulfill, custom orders, and all this food and desserts are going to waste because we only sell them fresh—it's just not right."

Cyril shrugged. "Police orders. You do know

that a murderer is on the loose here? I can't help that your patisserie happens to play yet another role in a murder. Call it bad luck, but we have to do our job."

Clémence got the urge, again, to smack the inspector silly. But she took a deep breath and turned to her staff. "I'm sorry, everyone. We'll call you back in when this ordeal is over. In the meanwhile, enjoy the morning off."

They filtered out, but Sebastien and Berenice lingered as Cyril's team got started.

"What a pain," said Berenice.

"Don't worry," said Clémence. "I know exactly what to do."

"What?" asked Sebastien.

"Call my mother," she said.

CHAPTER FOUR

*a*fter Clémence informed her parents, who were back in Tokyo after traveling around Japan, her mother called Cyril and gave him a piece of her mind. She said that if the store wasn't reopened by tomorrow, she'd have the country's best lawyers down Cyril's throat. She also threatened to bill him with the profit loss because there was no way any of her staff had anything to do with this.

She helped Caroline call and inform the customers with lunch reservations that the place would be closed for the day and that they would receive a fifty percent reduction for their next lunch. Then she put up two signs to inform walk-in customers of the closure, as well.

Clémence was so mad that she turned down lunch with Sebastien and Berenice. She went home to feed Miffy and tried to calm down.

In her bedroom bathroom, she took a lavender bubble bath and tried to relax. She thought about the dead man in the bush. He had died eating pistachio éclairs. They had been fresh éclairs, from what she could tell. It meant that they had been bought on the same day. There was no way that the staff would have had anything to do with this, on purpose or by accident. It wasn't as if they had bottles of poison just lying around.

But Clémence was worried. What if it was the éclairs? What if one of the bakers poured in something toxic by mistake, or some stranger had snuck in to do some damage? What if it was a competitor out to destroy their reputation?

Clémence splashed water on her face. She had to relax. She just had to wait for the results. When Cyril concluded that Damour had nothing to do with this death, the store would be reopened, and it would be business as usual.

She got out of the tub, ate lunch, and thought about how she could enjoy the rest of her day. It was an unexpected day off. If she were to hang out with Berenice and Sebastien, she would probably want to rant about Cyril, the whole situation, and get mad again. Maybe it was best for her to be alone and mellow out that day.

She decided to paint. She had set up an easel on the balcony earlier that week with the intention of painting again, but she never got around to it since she had been so busy at work. But her first love was art, after all. She did have great ambition to be a painter and put on her own show at a reputable art gallery someday.

Clémence had graduated from École Nationale Supérieure des Beaux-Arts, one of the best art schools in the country. She mainly studied the techniques of classical paintings. It had been a long, rigorous process, but she did it because she wanted to perfect the techniques of the masters so she would have the tools to develop her own style of painting.

What her style was, however, she didn't exactly know yet, even after all the years at school. She personally loved the impressionist paintings, cubism, and anything surreal. Recently, she'd been obsessed with the childlike whimsy in some of Marc Chagall's work.

For now, she would try to have fun with art again. To loosen herself up, she decided to sketch

Miffy. She sat down with a glass of wine and called Miffy out to the balcony.

It wasn't hard for Miffy to stay still. Clémence told her gently to sit, explaining that she was going to draw her in charcoal. Miffy smiled and wagged her tail as if she understood.

After an hour, she had five rough sketches of Miffy in various poses. She decided that she was ready to paint a portrait of Miffy.

It had to be good enough for her parents to want to frame and display in the apartment. The thought of that made Clémence hesitant with her paintbrush. Although she was proud to have graduated from one of the best art schools, she had never been considered the best in her class.

One of her professors used to tell her that her paintings were average and forgettable. She had been in awe of a couple of her classmates who were so talented and so sure of themselves. Clémence didn't have the same confidence when she held her brush. She hesitated, which was why she never made it as an artist. Plus, she hadn't really given it a good shot.

She was good at inventing pastries, and her skills could rival any top baker in Paris, but she'd learned that through osmosis. Her parents were the talented ones. It was in the blood. Baking, to her, was a lot simpler. It was a matter of picking and choosing ingredients and deciding which ones would work well together. The fun was in the "lab," the kitchen where she'd try and fail until she got the combination right. It was a lot of adjusting and patience.

So why couldn't she apply the same patience, certainty, and perseverance to her art? It was probably because she took it too seriously. Baking and experimenting in the kitchen was fun, while painting and trying to figure out what it was that she wanted to express through lines and colors was work. Painting conjured up insecurities, and it was easier to stick with what she was good at.

When she was living in Le Marais before she went on her two-year tour around the world, she had been the live-in girlfriend of a classmate, Mathieu, the one deemed "talented" in school. His technique did in fact rival the masters. His portraits of people were incredible.

The last she'd heard, Mathieu had put on a small exhibition, portraits of farmers from the countryside. She read one of the glowing reviews in the papers. As everyone had predicted, Mathieu was on his way. She wondered if he was still with the girl he'd broken up with her for, Susanne what's-her-name. He had scouted her from the streets and asked her to pose for one of his portraits. What a cliché it had been, the artist and the muse getting romantically involved.

The whole breakup had turned Clémence off from dating artists—and from creating art. After it happened, she decided to go off and travel, which had been one of the best decisions she'd ever made.

She'd been with Mathieu for three years, and she used to be crazy about him. Mathieu was so brilliant and charming, but ultimately, he didn't think Clémence was good enough for him. Looking back now, he had hardly been encouraging about her work. He was condescending toward her efforts, paying false compliments as if he was a parent praising the ugly scribbles of a child. There could only be one artist in a couple, and it certainly hadn't been Clémence.

"Oh, what the hell," she said to Miffy. "If I'm no good as a painter, I might as well just have fun with it, right? I already have a pretty good job. I'll just do it for the enjoyment of it."

Clémence looked up at la Tour Eiffel for moral support, which seemed to be emitting the positive response that she needed.

"If it sucks, I'll just throw the painting away, right? It's just practice."

Clémence went ahead and sketched Miffy on the canvas. She painted her on top of a Parisian rooftop, since that was her view from the balcony.

Time seemed to fly as she painted. Miffy barked every so often to cheer her on.

When Clémence took a break in the kitchen to eat a snack, she heard knocking at the kitchen door.

It was Ben, the Englishman who lived in one of the former servant rooms on the roof. He rented the room from her parents.

"Hey." The goofy Englishman was dressed all in black, his signature attire, and he was holding his laundry bag. "I saw that you were in, and I figured I'd be able to do the laundry. I tried calling you."

"Come on in. Sorry, I was on the balcony so I didn't hear the phone ring. Run the machine, and come have a drink outside if you want. I should go get my cell phone in case anyone else tries to call."

"Sure."

"Plus, I want to hear all the latest on your relationship with Berenice." Clémence smiled mischievously.

She had invited Berenice out to Ben's poetry slam a few weeks ago, and the two had hit it off.

"You're gonna grill me, are you? You're going to have to ply me with alcohol first."

"It's three o'clock in the afternoon," said Clémence. "Sometimes I worry about your drinking problem."

"Don't worry." Ben grinned. "It's just the British in me."

They took a bottle of white wine to share on the balcony. The sun was bright, and the clouds were a brilliant white.

"What's that you got there?" Ben peered at the half-finished painting on the easel. "You did this?"

"Just now," Clémence said, a little embarrassed. She'd been looking at the painting so closely that she had not stepped back to look at it in its entirety until now. She scrutinized it, hoping that it wasn't awful.

"It's amazing," Ben said.

"Really?" Clémence beamed. She did think the painting wasn't too bad. There was a sense of whimsy to it, and it captured Miffy's friendly personality well. "I'm still working on the shading."

"I'd forgotten that you were a painter," said Ben.

"I'm trying to get back into it," said Clémence.

"You're obviously very good."

Clémence blushed. Her parents had always told her that she was good, but art school had been so competitive. It felt good to have another person tell her that she had talent, even if he was a friend.

"Is that what you want to be? A painter? Your mother mentioned that you really wanted to be a great painter."

Clémence groaned. "She told you that? I suppose I do."

"So you're thinking of putting on a show any time soon?"

"A show? No, I'm just trying to practice."

"But that's the ultimate goal, right?"

"Well, I guess so," Clémence admitted.

"I have friends in Belleville," said Ben. "If you ever want to put on a small exhibition or something, I know some artists and gallery owners. Maybe you can team up with some other artists." His face lit up. "Or we can collaborate, too. We can make it an art and performance project. I can get my musician and dancer friends in on it, and we can perform all evening. Maybe we can put on a show where there's a performance every hour."

Clémence's head spun. She'd just wanted to draw her dog, and Ben wanted to put on some big spectacle?

"I wouldn't even know what to paint," said Clémence. "I'm still trying to find my footing."

"You're painting Miffy," said Ben.

"Yes, but I can't put on a show with portraits of my dog."

"Anything can be done, but you must paint something you're passionate about."

Clémence thought about it. "Well, I'm passionate about desserts."

"Yes, desserts! It's perfect! Clémence Damour of the Damour patisseries painting desserts and pastries. I'm sure people will snatch those pieces up."

She gave a little laugh. "Sounds like a big advertisement for our company."

"Not if it's sincere," said Ben. "Cheers."

They clinked wine glasses.

Clémence smiled. "You should be an inspirational speaker or something."

"I'm a writer," said Ben. "I help people with perspective."

"How's that mystery novel coming along?" asked Clémence.

"It's going well. The inspector has decoded the pages of code in the briefcase. I've decided that it's a plan to access another dimension. But now it's turning into sci-fi."

"A sci-fi mystery. Sounds cool. Berenice loves mysteries. You should let her read it."

Clémence turned to Ben, waiting for his response.

"She is reading it," said Ben. "She has plenty of ideas."

"So is it official now?" Clémence grinned. "Are you a couple?"

"I don't know," said Ben. "I really like hanging out with her, but I don't know if either of us are taking the romance aspect seriously, which makes me wonder if there is a romantic aspect. I mean, we're attracted to each other, and we have a good intellectual rapport, but I wonder if the chemistry is there."

"Well, have you tried to kiss her?"

"No," he said.

"No?" Clémence gaped. "What are you waiting for?"

"We only hang out once or twice a week. She doesn't seem to be in a rush. I think she might even be dating other guys, but I like her, so I'm waiting to see how this unfolds naturally."

Clémence shrugged. "Maybe that's a good idea."

Berenice was a little boy crazy. She often made eyes at Raoul, who worked at Damour. Still, it did seem as though she and Ben had a lot in common, but if one took the relationship more seriously than the other, someone could get hurt. Clémence would probably end up feeling responsible because she had been the one to introduce them, after all.

"But you're also right," said Ben. "A kiss would probably tell me if we have something more. If there isn't, we'll just go back to being friends, no big deal."

"You're very practical for a poet and a fiction writer," Clémence remarked.

"We're not all drunks and philanderers," Ben joked. "Don't you usually work at this time, or are you taking an extended lunch break?"

"Oh." Clémence sighed. "No. Actually, the place is closed for the day."

Clémence explained about the murder and the poisoned éclairs.

"That's really strange," said Ben. "Paris is actually a pretty sinister place, if you think about it."

"Don't blame Paris," said Clémence. "Blame

the psychopathic murderers. I wonder who would do such a thing."

"So the inspector thinks your store has something to do with it?"

"I think he hopes that it does," said Clémence. "He's out to get me."

"I think he's out to get everyone." Ben had met Cyril once and felt the same way about him that Clémence did.

"What if he finds something?" Clémence asked. "What if the store is responsible?"

Just then, the cell phone she'd taken out to the balcony with her began to ring on the table. An unknown number.

CHAPTER FIVE

"One of your staff members has been arrested," said Cyril.

"What?" Clémence exclaimed, jumping up.

"Raoul Baka. Just thought you would want to know."

Cyril hung up.

"I can't believe this!" Clémence said to Ben.

"What?"

"Apparently Raoul has something to do with this."

"Who's Raoul?"

"He's one of the cashiers at the patisserie. I've got to go to the store and chew off that inspector's head!"

Clémence went back inside the apartment.

"I'll go with you so you don't seriously hurt that inspector," Ben said.

They walked back to Place du Trocadéro, where Damour was. A few people gathered outside, looking into the window, wondering what was going on.

This was not good. This was not good at all. Not only was the store closed, her customers could see the police car and Cyril's team in the store. Now an employee had been arrested in connection with a murder. Her parents were going to be furious. Clémence's fear would be realized: Damour's reputation would take a nosedive under her watch. How could she let this happen?

She knocked on the door to the salon de thé. One of the members of Cyril's team opened up.

"Where is he?" she demanded. "Cyril St. Clair?"

At the sight of her furious face, the man didn't hesitate in pulling Cyril out of the back kitchen. Clémence stepped in the store with Ben. From outside, a camera flashed. People were taking pictures of this. They would be in the papers. What a mess.

Cyril had that smug grin on his face, with lines that appeared at the sides of his mouth like parentheses trying to contain his mean intentions. "Ah, Mademoiselle Damour. I knew it was only a matter of time before you started sticking your nose in our business again."

Clémence crossed her arms and bit back a retort about his large nose. She wasn't in grade school. Trading insults wasn't going to get her anywhere.

"What's the story?" she asked instead.

"It seems to me that your employee had a public spat with our deceased only a few days ago. A grocer saw him punch out Monsieur Dupont in front of his grocery. Plus, Raoul had been working the morning shift the day that Dupont was killed, so putting two and two together—it's simple mathematics, really."

"In this case, you end up with five," said Clémence. "It's circumstantial evidence, but did you even find any traces of poison or anything suspicious around here? Do you even have proof that Raoul poisoned the éclairs or know of any witnesses who'd seen him do it?"

"You are lucky that your employee covered his tracks well, but he still has a couple of eyewitnesses who saw him punch out Dupont on the street, as

I've told you. It explains why Dupont's eye still has a trace of a bruise."

"Who is this Dupont guy, anyway?" Ben asked.

"Alexandre Dupont," said Cyril. "One of your best éclair customers, according to his wife—who is in hysterics, by the way. He works at Avenue Kléber and comes to your patisserie often, though he's learned his lesson now, hasn't he?"

Cyril let out a nasty laugh. Clémence grimaced, disgusted by his ability to joke at a time like this.

Clémence had never seen Dupont at the store before, but she'd only been back for a month. Her employees probably knew way more about him. And she was eager to find out why Raoul would punch him out.

"Where is Raoul?" asked Clémence.

"Already in custody."

"Can I talk to him?"

"Not unless you're his lawyer."

She sighed. "So why did Raoul punch Dupont?" she asked Cyril.

"I don't know yet," said Cyril. "But I'll be questioning him later on. Next time, be careful who you hire."

"What about the store?" Clémence asked.

"You've found nothing, right? So can we reopen it now?"

"Yes, fine. You're lucky that my men are so fast."

"Fast? You've cost us a whole day of business! We pride ourselves on freshness, so some of the desserts are garbage now."

"If that's the case, why don't you give them to us?" Cyril said.

Clémence couldn't tell if he was joking. His expression was neutral, awaiting a response.

"You can't be serious! You expect me to give our gourmet desserts and pastries to you and your team as a reward for shutting down our store, arresting one of my employees with no real evidence, and insulting me?"

Cyril sputtered. "You did say the desserts were going to waste."

"What are you, pigeons? No, I'm not giving you anything!"

Ben had to stifle his laughter.

Cyril's face fell. "Fine. Our men are leaving soon. They've tested a good portion of your pastries for poison, so a lot of your food is already in the garbage, anyway."

"Whatever," said Clémence. "Now get out, all of you."

Some of the men who were still working turned to her with alarm.

"No need to be rude, Damour," said Cyril with an infuriating grin. "We're off. We got what we wanted. Just accept it. One of your employees is a cunning killer. Poisoning a customer like that. You'll be lucky this whole thing doesn't spread. People will avoid your store out of fear for their lives."

With that, Cyril turned and left the store. His men followed after gathering up their supplies, leaving the store a complete mess.

CHAPTER SIX

*C*lémence called Caroline. Together, they called back in many of their employees to help clean up the store. They were open almost as late as the other restaurants at Place du Trocadéro, so they could aim to reopen for dinner if they cleaned up in time.

While Cyril's team did throw a good portion of the food into the trash, there were still plenty left on the covered cooling trays. As the employees got to work, Clémence gathered up Caroline, Celine, and Marie in the employee lounge. Marie worked in the patisserie as a cashier. Celine was a hostess, as well as Clémence's friend.

"I didn't want to tell the others," Clémence

started, "but I have to let you know that Raoul has been arrested."

"Pourquoi?" Celine frowned in concern.

Clémence told them about the dead customer, Alexandre Dupont, and how Raoul had been seen arguing and fighting with him last week on the street.

"I'm just wondering what you know about Raoul and this Dupont guy," said Clémence. "C'est grave. It's very serious. Raoul might be tried for murder."

"That can't be," Marie exclaimed. "Raoul is a great guy."

"I agree," said Caroline. "Raoul is one of our best employees. He's friendly and smiles a lot. Customers have commented that his smile really brightens up their day when they buy their morning pastries. I can't believe he'd fight Dupont—and murder?"

"What else do you know about Raoul?" asked Clémence. "If we're going to clear his name, I need more of his background info, as well as Dupont's."

"He's from Marseille," said Caroline. "He likes working in the patisserie, but his real passion is music."

"He wants to be a music producer," said Marie. "He's already helping some new hip-hop artists in the studio, but not enough to make a living yet."

"Now, he lives in Courbevoie, near La Defense," Caroline added.

"What about the fight with Dupont?" Clémence asked. "Why would he do that? There were two eyewitnesses who saw him punch Dupont on the street."

"Dupont…Who is he?" Marie asked. "There are so many costumers, and we don't know them all by name."

Clémence tried to describe him the best she could—from what she could remember of the dead body, anyway.

"Is his top lip thinner than the bottom lip?" Marie asked.

"Yes," said Clémence.

"I do remember this guy. I don't like him. He doesn't say a lot, but he seems arrogant. I don't think Raoul liked him much, either."

"Why exactly? Did he ever say anything?"

"It was more his eyes," said Marie. "He had these pale blue eyes that were really cold. He'd only order by saying what he wanted, never a s'il vous plait."

"What would he usually order?"

"He liked the éclairs, mainly the pistachio ones. Sometimes he'd order the chocolate, or the salted caramel one, as well. Otherwise, he'd buy a pain au chocolat."

"I think I've seen him dine with his work colleagues in the salon de thé for lunch," said Celine. "But I'm not sure. You can't really pick this guy out of a crowd. He looks like every businessman in the area. I'm not sure why Raoul would fight with him. I wonder if he knew him personally."

"I want to ask him," said Clémence, "but he's detained right now. The police are grilling him. We've got to find out more about Dupont."

"We do have a video camera installed in the patisserie," said Caroline. "It's hidden in the chandelier."

"Really?"

Clémence went into the patisserie, and the girls followed. She looked up at the dazzling chandelier and couldn't see the camera.

"I can't believe it's up there," she said. "Did my parents install this recently?"

"A year ago," said Caroline. "It was long overdue."

"How do we replay the footage from yesterday?"

"There's a company in the fifteenth arrondisse-ment that we hire for our security," Caroline said. "The camera quality is not HD or anything, but we'd be able to see if this Dupont was here that day and whether Raoul had anything to do with this."

"Great! I wonder why that inspector didn't ask to see the store surveillance footage. Probably because he's so clueless. I'm going over there right now."

"I'll give you the card of the company," said Caroline, who then disappeared into the back office to get it.

Clémence took the Métro to Avenue Emile Zola. She'd made an emergency appointment with the surveillance company and knocked on the door of a storefront with dark tinted windows. A guy in his early thirties with scruffy facial hair answered the door.

"*Bonjour,*" Clémence greeted him. "Are you Monsieur Ralph Lemoine?"

"*Oui.* Clémence Damour?"

"That's me."

He let her in. The place was set up more like an apartment. The kitchen was at the front, with a living room that was really scattered with plenty of surveillance equipment, including TV screens and computers. There was a staircase that led to a floor upstairs.

Ralph was wearing scruffy jeans, sneakers, a ripped gray T-shirt, and a white hoodie. His brown eyes were rich in color, but his dark under-eye circles indicated that he hadn't slept much the night before.

"Do you live here, as well?" Clémence asked out of curiosity.

"Oh, no," said Ralph, "It's not an apartment, although I live in the neighborhood. There are a few other guys working upstairs, surveilling your stores and some other companies. I'm only dressed this way because we don't need to dress up for this job since we look at screens all day. Excuse me."

Ralph rubbed the back of his head sheepishly. In Paris, appearances were everything, but she knew how liberating it was to dress like a slob and not have to worry about what people thought. She had dressed in sweats during a good portion of her travels abroad.

Clémence smiled. "Don't apologize. You can dress however you want. I'm the one taking up your time."

"Do you want a café?" Ralph asked, moving near the espresso machine on the kitchen counter. He looked as though he needed one.

"Non, merci."

He made one for himself and sat down at the counter.

"So you're looking for someone on the surveillance tapes?" Ralph asked.

"Yes. This guy named Alexandre Dupont. I just want to look through the footage of Thursday morning to early afternoon. This is in the patisserie section of our store in the 16th."

"Sure," said Ralph. "Let me find it."

He went to his workspace, switched on a screen, and began typing on a keyboard. After a few minutes of fiddling, he was able to find the footage.

Clémence sat beside him as he started playing the footage at the beginning of the workday. The camera had a view of the profile of the customers in line, as well as the cashiers. She looked carefully at every man's face in the sped-up footage. After a couple of hours of reviewing each customer carefully, rewinding and freezing the footage at times, she shook her head.

"He wasn't there," she said. "Are you sure this footage is from yesterday?"

Ralph pointed to the date on the bottom right of the screen. "I'm one hundred percent sure."

"So this Dupont guy wasn't in the shop," Clémence said.

"If you don't recognize him, then he wasn't."

"Apparently he had bought two pistachio éclairs," Clémence said.

If Dupont hadn't bought the éclairs himself, someone else must have bought them for him that morning.

Cyril had mentioned that Dupont ate two pistachio éclairs. He could tell because of the glazing smeared inside the bag. There was no receipt to go with the purchase, but they had to have been bought in the morning—the nub of the éclair on the ground that Clémence had inspected had been fresh indeed, judging by the texture, by the shine on the glazing.

Besides, Damour never sold day-old pastries. Everything had to be fresh.

She had an idea. She would just have to find out

who had purchased two pistachio éclairs from their cash register. After thanking Ralph for his time, she grabbed her coat and immediately headed back to the patisserie.

CHAPTER SEVEN

The employees at Damour had done a good job of getting the patisserie back in shape. When Clémence walked in through the door, the counters were filled halfway up with fresh macarons, éclairs, tarts, croissants, and their other signature desserts and pastries. The staff for the evening shift had already arrived, and Caroline said that they could reopen soon.

Clémence asked Caroline and Marie to help her dig up all the purchases and transaction information on their cash register before the store opened.

"I want to know who bought two pistachio éclairs that morning," Clémence said. "If you can recall their names or faces, that would be great, but either way, I'll take the time of the transaction and go back to our surveillance guy to match the time the purchase was made to the video, so we can put a face to the purchase."

Caroline punched in her manager code on the touch screen of the cash register. With a few more punches of the keys, she was able to print out a long receipt of all the transactions made on Thursday. While it printed, Clémence turned to Marie.

"Do you always choose the right flavors when you're ringing up, say a pistachio éclair versus a chocolate éclair?"

"Yes," she replied. "We all do. It's how we determine which flavors are more popular."

"Which éclairs are more popular, anyway?" Clémence asked.

"The salted caramel and the chocolate are neck and neck," said Marie. "But pistachio and passion fruit are popular, as well."

"Are there any customers who buy two pistachio éclairs on a regular basis?"

"Hmm, I don't know. Sometimes it happens, I suppose, but people buy all sorts of combinations. It's hard to keep track."

When the receipts finished printing, Clémence turned her attention to it. Numerous éclairs had been bought that morning, but they weren't as popular as croissants, *pains au chocolat*, and other pastries and breads for the morning crowd. Single éclairs had been bought, but two?

After she went through all the purchases, she found out that there had only been three transactions that included two pistachios purchased at the same time.

Clémence called Ralph again, saying she was coming back and needed more of his help.

Ralph opened the door, but he had changed clothes. Instead of his casual sweats, he was wearing khakis, a striped blue dress shirt, and brown dress shoes. Gone was his facial hair, and his hair had been combed.

He smiled, and a dimple appeared on his left cheek that Clémence hadn't noticed before when he had the scruffy facial hair.

"I decided to go home and change," he said.

"What made you do that?" Clémence asked.

"In case another beautiful woman comes in to see me today," he said, looking into her blue eyes.

Clémence blushed.

He did look handsome, all cleaned up. He stood

up straighter, too, and Clémence could tell that he was in good shape, from what his well-fitted dress shirt revealed.

She hadn't paid much attention to him before, but she appreciated his effort in looking good for her. She was in a white oversized cashmere sweater that hung nicely on her thin frame, black python-print leggings, and black ankle boots. The outfit was chic enough, but not exactly something to inspire men. She couldn't take his flirtations seriously, however. Many men were incorrigible flirts.

She got down to business and asked him for help in finding the footage for the three transaction times.

As he had before, Ralph found her account on his system, and rewound the footage for the first transaction, at 8:13 a.m. It was a little boy, around ten years old. He wore a helmet with a frog on it. Clémence dismissed it and told Ralph to find the second time, which as at 8:47 a.m. The customer was a tall businessman. He looked to be in his early thirties, but she could be wrong, since the screen quality wasn't the best.

Clémence asked Ralph to pause when he looked in the direction of the camera. She remembered his face but took a picture of the screen with her cell phone for good measure. She would show it to her staff and ask whether they recognized this guy.

The third transaction was from a lady who looked like a fashionable bourgeois housewife with too much time on her hands. She ordered a huge box of treats, along with the pistachio éclairs. It couldn't have been her. The éclairs found on Dupont came in Damour's lavender paper bag.

The little boy and the woman didn't seem like possible suspects. Her biggest lead was the businessman, who surely worked in the area. Clémence had to find out just how he was connected to Dupont.

CHAPTER EIGHT

"*I* do know him," said Celine incredulously.

Back in the employee section of the patisserie, Clémence had shown her the picture on her smartphone. Berenice and Marie were there, as well, getting ready to leave at the end of their shifts. They'd all been working longer than usual, but the store was reopened, and things were more or less back to normal.

"I've seen him too," said Marie. "Although he only started coming in recently."

"He's pretty good looking," said Celine.

Berenice craned her neck to look at the fuzzy picture on Clémence's phone. "I suppose he does have good bone structure."

"Really, guys?" Clémence said, amused. "We're talking about a potential murderer here. And I don't think he's all that cute."

"No, he's really charming," said Celine. "Green eyes, dirty blond hair, and this pouty lower lip like Brad Pitt's. He looks better in person, trust me."

"He's American," said Marie. "At least, I recall him speaking French with an American accent, if I'm not mistaken."

"You're probably right," said Celine. "He stumbles on his words a little, which makes him even more adorable. I'm pretty sure he came in for lunch one day with a colleague. They were both in suits, but I noticed him because of his build." Celine sighed dreamily.

"I don't think he's *that* good looking," said Marie. "I see what you're saying about the pouty lips, but his eyes were kind of pale and cold."

"No way," said Celine. "He was really smiley and friendly. He didn't look cold at all."

"I just meant his eyes," said Marie.

"Are they the eyes of a killer?" Berenice asked in her mischievous way.

Marie shrugged. "Maybe. But I guess it's not a crime to have light-colored eyes."

"He's too hot to be a killer," said Celine. "He's

tall, he's got nice broad shoulders, and I think he works out."

Clémence shook her head. Hot men were always the topic of conversation with her employees. "Let's get back on track here. What else do you know about him? Where does he work?"

Marie shrugged. "Not sure. We never had time to chat or anything. You know what it's like during the morning rush."

"I don't know, either," said Celine. "His colleague was French, as I recall."

"Maybe we can trace his credit card or something," said Clémence. "Although he did pay for his éclairs in cash. Maybe he paid for his lunch in cash, as well."

"He might be coming in tomorrow," said Marie. "Why don't you wait for him then? He's been in consistently for the past few days now, probably before he goes to work."

"Okay," said Clémence. "I'll do that, then. I'll be here early in the morning, and I'll wait for him. Now let's go. Go home, and get some rest. I'll see you tomorrow, then."

As Clémence walked back home from work in the early evening, it started to rain. Not just light rain, but a great downpour. In Paris, the weather could change in an instant. The clouds were fast moving; the sky, temperamental.

Clémence remembered that she had left her painting of Miffy on the balcony.

"Oh, no." She raced back home. The painting might've been ruined.

She entered her building and waited impatiently for the small elevator to come down. When the doors of the elevator opened, Arthur came out with Youki.

"Bonsoir," he said.

"Oh, hello," said Clémence. "You're walking Youki in this weather?"

"Actually, I have to run some errands," he said. "And Youki's not afraid of a bit of water."

"Well, see you later then."

Arthur frowned, scrutinizing her. "Are you okay?"

"Yes. Why wouldn't I be?"

"You seem a little haggard and run down."

Clémence frowned. "What do you mean?"

"Tired," said Arthur. "Your complexion is muddy, and your eyes are bloodshot."

"What are you saying?" Clémence was getting more angry by the second.

"That you probably need some rest," said Arthur. "Why are you getting mad?"

"Are you absolutely clueless? You don't tell a girl that she looks horrible."

"I didn't say horrible. I said 'run down.'"

"And 'haggard.' It's been a long day, okay? I'm not just sitting around all day picking lint out of my belly button."

Arthur smiled, amused by how easily she got riled up.

"What's going on, anyway?" said Arthur. "I noticed Damour was closed this morning."

Clémence sighed. She was tired, and she didn't feel like talking about the situation with Arthur. Besides, what good could come out of it, anyhow? It wasn't as if he would be able to help.

"Nothing," she said. "Just some technical problems. We're back and running now. If you'll excuse me, I have to go home."

"Okay, *bonne soirée*. See you around."

Clémence pressed the fifth floor button, hoping the door would close sooner. She didn't want to talk to anyone else, especially Arthur. How clueless he was, to tell her that she looked haggard. The boy could be so incredibly insensitive that it was laughable. Every time she started warming up to him, he would say something off-putting.

Clémence wasn't entirely innocent, either. She didn't know why she made that comment about belly button lint. She supposed she was just grasping at straws to insult Arthur right back. When was he going to move out of the building, already? She had run into him two days in a row now.

When she went home and ran out to the balcony to retrieve her painting, it had already been pelted by the rain.

"Oh great." Clémence shook her head.

Miffy was at her feet, barking at the canvas in her hand. Some of the paint had smudged a bit.

"I'm sorry, Miffy. Looks like I'll have to take some time to fix this."

She took a couple of dishrags from the kitchen cabinet and placed the canvas on top of them on the counter.

Under the bright lights of the kitchen, she looked at the painting more closely. The more she looked at it, the more she liked it. The rain had ruined some of her detailing and given it a gauzy effect—really runny in some areas, but still clear in others. She liked this particular style. It gave her a distinctive feeling that this was what life was like in Paris: crystal clear and beautiful, yet dreamy and gauzy, even messy.

Although she wouldn't try to pelt her oil paints with any more rainwater, she would play with this type of experimental texture in her future work— on purpose, this time. It wouldn't be a bad idea. Not everything had to be perfect and anatomically correct all the time, the way she had been taught all those years in art school.

She could take Ben's advice and paint what she was passionate about. Desserts and pastries could be incorporated. Clémence had a few ideas about what she could do, but it had been a very long day and she didn't have the energy to dwell on them.

Clémence gave Miffy a kiss and began to make spaghetti Bolognese for dinner. It was fast and easy, and she just wanted to eat and get some rest.

As she waited for the water to boil, she looked into the mirror at her reflection. It was true that she wasn't looking her freshest. She had dark under-eye circles, and her skin was paler than usual. But *haggard*?

She refused to be insecure about it. She was human. She couldn't look beautiful all the time.

And if a jerk like Arthur couldn't accept that, well, she didn't need to talk to him. Ever.

Why did she have to give so much weight to what boys said? On the same day, Ralph had called her beautiful, and Arthur had said she'd looked horrible. Maybe she should be the one to decide whether she looked beautiful or not.

Right now, beauty should've been the last thing on her mind. She needed to eat, and she needed rest. She had a murder case to solve.

CHAPTER NINE

When Clémence went into work the next morning, Sebastien had already finished making a tray of their newest éclair flavor. He'd been piping in the cream when she came in, and he handed one to her.

"Try it," said Sebastien. "And give it to me straight."

"When do I ever not?" asked Clémence.

She took a bite. The pastry was still a bit warm, and the cream filling fresh. She almost moaned in pleasure, but she restrained herself.

"What did you do?" she said. "This is amazing."

Sebastien crossed his arms and smiled proudly.

"You said you wanted a hazelnut flavor, so you got it."

"But there's something else that's going well with this. What is it?" Clémence took another bite. "Orange?"

Sebastien nodded.

"It tastes so fresh," said Clémence. "You're a genius."

Sebastien smiled and flushed with pride. "I knew you'd go crazy for it."

"Get over yourself." Clémence groaned. "We can launch this flavor next week. Give me the recipe, and I'll send it off to the bakers in the other locations."

"Even Tokyo and Hong Kong?" Sebastien asked, referring to the two new patisseries that had opened recently in Asia.

"We'll see," said Clémence. "I'll send the recipe to my parents, and they can decide if it'll do well for the market. Right now they're still doing market research and collecting information on what's doing well and what's not. I'm not sure if they'll want new flavors so soon, but I'll ask them."

"So my experimental savory flavored éclairs will just have to wait, too, huh?"

"Yes," said Clémence. "We'll see if it works in Paris first. Simon really liked it though." She referred to the head chef in charge of the menu for the salon de thé. "We'll have to see if there's enough demand for it to be featured permanently on the menu."

"It should do well," Sebastien said confidently.

"Probably," said Clémence. "But is it possible for your head to get any bigger?"

"No, it's not," he replied dryly.

His sister came in.

"Hey, Berenice," said Clémence. "Any sight of that guy in the patisserie?"

"Nope, but when Marie calls you, I want to come out, too. I want to see just how hot this guy really is."

"What guy?" asked Sebastien.

"The potential murderer," Berenice said.

"*What?*"

Clémence had to explain how she found out about this guy through their surveillance company.

"I didn't know we had surveillance." Sebastien looked around the kitchen. "Are we being filmed right now?"

"You didn't know about the cameras?" said Berenice. "It's up there, see?"

Berenice pointed to a black dome on the high ceiling.

"Oh," said Sebastien. "I thought that was some sort of light or something. High tech."

"I hope you're not doing anything here you shouldn't be doing," Clémence teased.

"Of course not," Sebastien said.

"I'd like to install some cameras in your apartment." Berenice turned to Clémence. "I never know what he's up to. Even when he was still living with us, Sebastien would just hide out in his room all the time."

"I need time to myself," Sebastien said. "It doesn't mean I'm doing anything weird."

"Yes, but you're always so private, even to your family. We always get this impression that you're hiding something."

"You guys are just too nosy," said Sebastien. "You and Mom. Maybe I just don't want to give you a play-by-play of everything I'm doing during my day."

"Take, for example, Tuesday and Thursday nights," said Berenice. "Where do you go? We notice that you don't ever answer your phone around that time. Do you have a girlfriend now or what?"

"That's none of your business," said Sebastien.

"If you're seeing someone, you'll have to present her to us, you know."

"Why?"

"Don't you care what we think?"

"No," said Sebastien.

"So you *are* seeing someone?" Berenice asked.

"I didn't say that, either."

Berenice gave an exaggerated sigh. "See? You can't get anything out of this guy. He doesn't even have Facebook or any kind of online presence."

"Well, I don't have Facebook, either," said Clémence.

"You don't?" Sebastien gave her a high five.

"Sometimes I post on the Damour fan page," said Clémence. "So I'm not entirely social network-free."

"That's different if you're just using it for business," said Sebastien. "But I don't really care what people eat for lunch or other mundane status updates, you know?"

"Unless they're eating at Damour," said Clémence. "But I get what you're saying. I'd rather get to know people face-to-face."

Clémence used to have a Facebook profile, but she deleted it when she started seeing photos of her ex Mathieu with his new girlfriend. She had been so distraught that she blocked him. Still, his pictures showed up in the feeds of their mutual friends, and she just had to delete her profile altogether and start living in the real world by taking off for her travels. She didn't miss being online one bit.

"You're just as hard to get to know offline," Berenice said to Sebastien. "As your sister, how am I suppose to give you guidance on relationships if I don't know what you're up to?"

"Maybe I don't need your guidance," Sebastien retorted.

Clémence shook her head at the brother and sister. They looked alike, but they were so different. It made her miss her older brother and sister, who were living outside of Paris. Her brother was in Deauville in Normandy, and her sister was in the south of France. She hadn't seen Henri and Marianne since her birthday in January, when they'd all visited her in Malaysia.

"I very much doubt it," said Berenice. She turned back to Clémence again. "Did you know that Seb was in a relationship for three years, and I didn't even know it until two years in? I ran into them at the movies once and that was when I found out."

"You're really annoying me," said Sebastien. "I'm not one of you girls. I don't kiss and tell."

Clémence laughed. They could spend entire lunch hours talking about boys with Clémence. But she understood Sebastien's discretion. Lately she'd been guarded about her love life, too, although there wasn't much to talk about to begin with.

Celine came into the kitchen. *"Pssst,"* she called to Clémence.

Clémence walked to her. "What is it?"

"He's here," Celine said in a loud stage whisper. "Your main man."

"The murderer guy?" Berenice asked.

"Yes. He's in line right now. I just saw him walk past the door and into the patisserie."

They turned to Clémence.

"What are you going to say?" Sebastien said.

"I think I'm just going to follow him for now," said Clémence. "I don't want him to know that I work here."

"Own the place you mean," Berenice said.

"I'll follow him to his workplace, see what he does, and I'll figure out how to talk to him after that."

"Clémence, come on," said Sebastien. "If this guy has killed someone, you have to be careful."

"I am careful," she said. "I'm not following him into alleys. It's Friday morning. It's safe."

Celine went back to her post. Clémence took off her apron and checked herself in a small mirror on the wall before she went out. The *salon de thé* was already full with customers eating breakfast. She traversed over to the patisserie section, which was divided by a half-wall. She could see the man's back. Marie and another cashier, Charlotte, were working, and Marie gave her a meaningful look. Clémence inched closer to get a better view. The man was looking at all their treats under the glass display.

He was looking at the éclairs, then the croissants. She was sure it was him, because he was the only man in a business suit in line.

Clémence waited, watching him from behind the wall opening. He ordered a *pain au chocolat*. As he paid, Clémence got ready to follow, but someone else came in through the patisserie door.

At the sight of her, this new arrival called out her name.

It was Arthur.

CHAPTER TEN

"*C*lémence!"

Startled, Clémence ducked back into the *salon de thé*. She hoped that her suspect hadn't spotted her.

"Hey, Clémence." Arthur came through to the salon section with a puzzled look. "Didn't you see me?"

Clémence shushed him. "Stop calling my name," she said in a loud whisper. "What are you doing here, anyway?"

"I wanted to talk to you," said Arthur.

Clémence snuck another look into the patisserie.

"He's leaving!" she exclaimed.

She watched the man push the door open and turn the corner.

"Who's leaving?" Arthur asked.

"Never mind." She moved toward the door. She should follow at a good distance behind. "Arthur, this is not a good time."

She pushed the door open.

"You're not seriously stalking some guy, are you?" Arthur said. He came out after her.

Clémence groaned. "No. I mean yes, okay, I am following someone, but it's not what you think."

"How do you know what I think?" He was walking next to her now, as Clémence turned onto Avenue Raymond-Poincaré.

"Don't you have somewhere to be?" Clémence asked.

Arthur was carrying a briefcase. "Yes, I was going to go to the library to work on my thesis, but I thought I'd stop by and talk to you first."

"*Pourquoi?* What do you want to talk about?"

"I'll tell you if you tell me what exactly it is that you're doing following some guy in the early morning."

Clémence sighed. He could be quite persistent when he wanted to be. "Fine. I'm trying to solve another murder case, all right?"

"Oh. Don't tell me it's for the guy we found in the bush."

Clémence nodded. She gave him the quick rundown of what she'd found out so far.

"If he's been coming in the store consistently, doesn't it mean that he just likes your baked goods?" Arthur asked.

"He's my biggest lead, so I have to check this out. What if he poisons someone else?"

"This is insane. You've already gotten seriously injured the last time you tried to find a murderer."

"Yes, but I found out who the murderer was, didn't I?" Clémence didn't know why Arthur had to be so argumentative. "Now I've told you what I'm up to. What did you want to tell me?"

Before he could answer, the man went inside a bank. It wasn't the bank that Clémence was a client of, but she wondered if he worked there, or whether he was just there to make a transaction.

"Act casual," Clémence said. "Pretend we're just walking by and I'm going to look inside the window to see if the guy's there."

"Fine."

They walked by, but Clémence didn't see him. The receptionist was sitting at the front desk, and there were no one else in sight, not even clients.

"I'm going to have to go in to find out," said Clémence.

Before Arthur could object, Clémence went into the bank. The attractive receptionist greeted her, and Clémence smiled back, but she moved to the cash machine. She would make a withdrawal. If the man didn't reappear, it meant either that the man worked there, or that he had an appointment.

She should have followed him in immediately. She would've been able to tell from how the receptionist greeted him whether he was a client or an employee. That Arthur really set back her investigation.

By the time the euros came out of the ATM, the man still hadn't appeared. Clémence considered asking the receptionist. But the receptionist might refuse to tell her who the man was if she didn't have a good reason to know.

When she went back outside, Arthur was still hanging around, waiting.

"Why are you still here?" she asked him.

"I have better things to do, obviously," he replied haughtily. "But you've made it difficult."

"I'm making your life difficult? You've just set my investigation back." Clémence explained that she had to wait around now for the man to come back out.

"Okay, Clouseau, I didn't mean to." Arthur's

face softened. "Come on. Let's just go across the street, and I'll buy you a drink."

Clémence wanted to reject his offer because she didn't want to spend any more time with him, but this made the most sense. The café across the street did have a solid view of the bank, and she'd be able to keep an eye on the scene without appearing suspicious.

"Fine," she said.

They went in and sat down, and Arthur flagged down the server.

"Un café, s'il vous plait," Clémence ordered.

"Make that two," Arthur said.

"What did you want to talk about anyway?" she asked.

"I just came over to give you an apology," said Arthur.

"Why?" Clémence was suspicious. Arthur apologizing? Surely there was a catch.

She turned and looked into his eyes. Arthur stared back. His brown eyes almost looked tender in the sunlight. And he seemed a little nervous.

"I think I offended you yesterday with my comment about you looking…run down."

Clémence raised an eyebrow. "Really?" she asked dryly.

"Yes, I mean, I personally can't understand why, but I suppose women are sensitive to these things."

"I was not offended," Clémence said. "I was annoyed."

"Fine, which is why I'm apologizing."

Clémence wondered why Arthur cared. He was rude to her half of the time. His behavior was quite inconsistent, but she had to give him credit for at least owning up to part of his rudeness.

"I accept your apology."

"Okay," Arthur said, looking satisfied.

The waiter arrived with their espressos.

"If you want to go soon, you can," said Clémence. "I'll just sit here and wait."

"Well, we found the body together. We might as well wait for the killer together."

Clémence gave a laugh. "You want to join in on the sleuthing?"

"Look, you're poking around a guy who's a potential killer. You need someone as backup."

"I don't need backup."

"Oh, for the last time—I found you unconscious a month ago, remember?"

"I didn't really plan that evening," said Clémence. "I just happened to have been home very late and things happened."

"Exactly," said Arthur. "Sometimes you don't think. You just act. Somebody has to be the voice of reason."

"And you think that's your voice?" Clémence shook her head.

"You're impossible," Arthur said. "I'm just trying to keep you from getting killed."

"If I need help, I'll ask for it."

What was it about Arthur that always brought out her argumentative side? If she really needed protection, she had plenty of guy friends to ask, like Ben or Sebastien, and she wanted to tell him that, but something stopped her.

She looked at Arthur. Did she find him attractive? Sure, objectively, but was she personally romantically interested in him? She couldn't be. Especially after he'd sneered about the flowers when she'd asked, or his insensitive insults, even if he'd just apologized.

He ran a hand through his hair in frustration. "Let's talk about something else."

"Fine."

"I hear you're a painter," he said.

"I dabble," she said. "Why? Did your mother mention it?"

"Yes."

Clémence got the feeling that Arthur's mother really wanted him to pursue her. She also knew, however, that Arthur was more into bimbos. She'd seen enough girls coming out of the building with him on Sunday mornings—girls in tight miniskirts and salacious curves doing the walk of shame. In fact, he had been bringing one of these girls home late at night when he'd found her unconscious outside of their building, over a month ago.

So why was he being so nice now? Surely she wasn't his type. She was slim and dark haired—not curvaceous and blond like his usual type. She didn't show much skin at all.

Clémence couldn't go out with someone with such superficial taste in women. She'd been heartbroken by someone who'd dumped her for a great beauty, and she wasn't going to risk her heart again. Especially by someone who was in essence a spoiled rich kid, even if he was working on a PhD and living in a servant's room.

Nevertheless, she indulged him in his inquiries about her art, answering his questions about what she'd studied in school and the artists who inspired her. Although she was surprised by his interest, she didn't want to delve into the subject of the personal paintings she was working on, or planned to work on. For now she felt like a fraud, a wannabe, even though she had a fancy degree.

Her ex-boyfriend had been the real artist. She knew she should probably have more confidence in herself, but confidence was something she had to build in this field.

She changed the subject to something that she'd been curious about, but had refrained from asking out of respect. But since Arthur seemed more and more relaxed, it felt like a good time to ask.

"Did your mother ever find out about Lana?" she asked.

He blew air out of his mouth and shrugged. "She probably knows, but I don't know for sure."

Last month, when Clémence had been investigating the murder of *la gardienne*, the caretaker of their building, she'd uncovered that Arthur's father had been having an affair with one of their maids. Arthur had been pretty upset about it. The maid immediately moved out from her room on the top floor. Such behavior from his father didn't surprise him.

"It doesn't really matter," Arthur continued. "Their marriage is not really built on love, you know?"

Clémence didn't. Her parents' love story was

grand and passionate. They'd met in culinary school, started the patisserie together, and to this day, they were still in love and having a great time traveling and having new adventures together.

"That's a shame," said Clémence.

Arthur shrugged again, as if to shrug the whole thing off. "It's peaceful at home right now, so that's all I can ask for."

Clémence looked at his profile. Strong chin, gold reflecting from his chestnut hair and tawny skin. He looked vulnerable enough that she felt the urge to hug him. An urge that she obviously resisted. Who knew when he was going to go back to being callous again? She couldn't open herself to that kind of vulnerability.

As she looked away, Arthur looked at her. She felt his gaze on her. Their faces were only inches away, and she wondered if he was inspecting her pores, her flaws.

She downed her café. How much longer did she have to sit there with him?

After another half hour of chatting about this and that, the man came out of the bank.

"There he is," Clémence exclaimed.

CHAPTER ELEVEN

The man lit a cigarette and took a call on his phone. From afar, Clémence couldn't decide whether he was handsome or not, as Celine had claimed. He was just as out of focus as the photo on her phone.

Although Clémence didn't know why it mattered how good-looking he was. She was spending way too much time with her boy-crazy employees.

"If he's taking a smoke break, he probably does work at the bank," Arthur said.

Clémence got up and searched her purse for her wallet to pay for her espresso.

"Let me." Arthur paid their bill.

Clémence thanked him, surprised. He could be

nice when he wanted to be. The nice thing about bourgeois boys was that they were raised to be gentlemen, even if they didn't behave all the time.

"What are you going to do?" he asked.

She watched the man, who was chatting away on the phone and paying no attention in their direction.

"I'm just going to find out who he is," she said. She stood up to cross the street.

By the time she made it across in the mad traffic, the man was already going back inside. He smoked like a Parisian. Parisian smokers were fast, sucking on those cigarettes as if they kept them alive.

"You're not going to follow me inside, are you?" she asked Arthur.

"Fine. I'll be waiting outside."

"Really, you can leave. You've wasted enough of your morning. Go work on your thesis."

Arthur groaned. "Just accept my help. I'll be out here like a bodyguard. I won't interfere with your schemes, whatever they are, okay?"

Clémence watched him closely. "All right."

She went inside the sliding doors of the bank, and the brunet receptionist greeted her again.

"*Bonjour.* Can I help you with something?"

"Yes," said Clémence. "I would like to make an appointment with one of your bankers."

"Okay, which one?"

Clémence couldn't believe she was going to do this, but it was the only plan she had. She lowered her voice. "The handsome one who just came back in from his cigarette break?"

"Ah," the receptionist was surprised, but soon her face fell into the knowing smile that women put on when they conspired with each other. "I see. He's certainly good-looking, isn't he?"

Clémence laughed in embarrassed. "Do you know if he's single?"

"As far as I know," said the receptionist. "If I wasn't married, I'd be after him, myself."

"I'm not a client here," said Clémence, "but if you tell me his name, I will be."

"John Christopher," she said. "He's American. He speaks fluent French, though, and he's our newest financial advisor. Did you want to make an appointment?"

"Yes," said Clémence. She was wealthy enough to make investments, if it came to that.

At that moment, however, John walked out to speak to the receptionist. The receptionist nodded toward Clémence.

"She's interested in your services." She turned to Clémence. "I'm sorry. I didn't catch your name?"

"Anabelle."

She had panicked and spat out the first name that came to mind, but she should've given her real name, especially if she was supposed to be starting some sort of account at this bank.

"*Bonjour*, Anabelle," John said in American-accented French. He introduced himself and smiled at her broadly. "Would you like to step inside my office? I have some time now, as a matter of fact."

Clémence inwardly panicked. This was turning awkward. She was just supposed to get his name and get out. But the man was in front of her now. And yes, Celine was right. He was certainly handsome, with his tanned skin, ocean green eyes, strong shoulders, and dirty blond hair. Americans weren't known for their suits, which were boxy, but he was in an expensive European-cut black suit, which accentuated all the right places. His smile wasn't too bad either.

She nodded and went in. *Merde*. What was she supposed to do now?

"Do you already have an account with us?" John asked.

"Er, yes."

"What's your last name, if I may ask?"

John was position in front of a computer, ready to key in her fake name. It was time to change directions.

"Actually," Clémence said. "I'm afraid I'm here under false pretenses. I'm not actually interested in starting an account or investments at all."

John frowned. "Oh?"

"You see, well, I saw you across the street, and I found you incredibly handsome." Clémence turned red as she said this. Nevertheless she kept a grin on her face, one she hoped was seductive.

She was no good at acting, but John seemed to be buying it. A cocky smile began to spread on his face.

"Wow. I didn't know French women could be so forward. I'm incredibly flattered."

"I don't usually do this," said Clémence. "But there was just something about you."

John beamed. His face softened, and he looked at her with more interest. "Would you like to go to dinner tomorrow night?"

He was American, and Americans didn't waste time.

"Yes," Clémence said.

John took her number and said he'd find a good restaurant and would call her as soon as he did.

When Clémence came out, the receptionist gave her the same conspiring smile.

"Tout va bien?" she asked. "It went well?"

Clémence nodded and smiled back weakly. She thanked her and went out the door. Her head felt light.

What had she done?

Did she just agree to go on a date with a potential murderer?

CHAPTER TWELVE

When Arthur asked her what had happened, she simply said that she'd found out his name and position. She didn't tell him about the hot date. For one, he would probably think that she was crazy.

Not that she cared about Arthur's approval—she simply didn't want him lecturing her again about putting herself in another potentially dangerous situation. She knew the risks involved. But it was just a date. John didn't know her true identity, and meeting him this way could work in her favor. Under the pretense of a date, she would find out more about him.

Plus, now that she knew his name, she could find out more about him. The sooner, the better.

Raoul was still being detained. After parting ways with Arthur, she walked back home and called her mother to find out more about what was happening with Raoul and their lawyers.

"I don't believe they have too much on him," her mother said. "Sure, there were eyewitnesses, but if there are no videos of Raoul giving Monsieur Dupont the éclairs that supposedly killed him, that should work in Raoul's favor. The problem is, they can't disprove it, either. Suppose they claim that Raoul gave him the éclairs outside of work."

Clémence sighed. "I'd like to talk to Raoul. How can I?"

"One of my lawyers is supposed to see him this afternoon. Why don't you go with him?"

"Okay, great," said Clémence. "Please put us in touch."

"I'll give him a call right away, dear, then I'll call you back. Imagine, another murder, and in connection with one of our employees, too. This is madness."

"Everything will be fine," said Clémence. She didn't want her mother to worry. "Just have a good time in Asia. Did you have a good time at the hot spring?"

"Yes, but I had the murder on my mind. I

know the store is up and running now, but I worried that there might be something in the papers?"

"Well, I didn't see anything in the papers this morning," said Clémence. In fact, she did see something on a gossip blog, but she didn't mention it to her mother. The blogger didn't seem to know much, anyway. The post had just mentioned that Damour was abruptly closed that morning and police had been spotted. It speculated theft, but not murder. They were lucky.

"Good," said her mother.

"I think we're fine for now. I'm working on it. I think there is someone else in connection with Dupont, but I have to find out more."

"I trust you, Clémence. You did figure out who killed la gardienne. Just be careful."

"Thanks, *maman.*"

Her mother didn't know how much danger Clémence had been in before she solved la gardienne's murder last month. And she wasn't going to tell her. If she did, her parents would fly back right away and be worried for no reason.

So last time Clémence had been careless, but this time, she would definitely be more on her guard. Be in public places and not alone with potential suspects. She should also probably take some more self-defense classes.

At home, she played with Miffy a bit. Miffy's portrait was still in the kitchen, drying on the dishrags. She propped it up against the wall and stepped back to look at it from different angles. It wasn't half bad. Miffy's face was mostly still intact and detailed.

She snacked on some madeleines and did some research on her laptop. She searched for John Christopher. There were several John Christophers on LinkedIn, but she found the right one fairly quickly since she knew where he worked.

John Christopher had an MBA from Stanford University. He spoke fluent English and French, and an adequate level of Spanish. He even put in the hobbies he enjoyed: swimming, tennis, and running. A normal guy—if normal meant a superior education on top of being athletic and generally good-looking. No wonder the other girls were crazy about him.

She wondered if other girls had been as forward as she had been, asking him out point-blank. Maybe he was used to girls hitting on him and giving him their phone numbers. He had been right—French girls were never forward. They were coy and coquettish. American girls were probably more blunt.

Clémence stopped her line of thinking. What was she doing? This was a murder investigation. She had to get focused.

She searched next for Alexandre Dupont on LinkedIn. Perhaps they'd worked together. However, the search came back with more than a dozen hits, and none of them seemed to be the right guy. Maybe Dupont didn't have LinkedIn. A broad Internet search didn't show what she wanted either. It would've been easier if she knew more about Dupont, like where he worked. That way she would be able to narrow down her search.

Clémence met the lawyer outside of 36 Quai des Orfèvres. Michel Martinez was a kind-looking man in his late fifties, with a friendly smile and salt and pepper hair. He wore round spectacles and carried a black briefcase.

They introduced themselves and shook hands. Michel came recommended by her parent's lawyers.

Her parents had known Raoul for over two years and didn't doubt his upstanding character.

The police, however, were taking forever to figure this out. Cyril didn't like to be wrong, and Clémence knew that it would take some convincing for him to let Raoul off the hook.

Clémence was dressed in a black pantsuit. She hoped to pass as Michel's associate so they would let her speak to Raoul.

On the third floor, Clémence and Michel waited to be called in. After twenty minutes, they were shown in to a room where Raoul was sitting at a small table.

"Clémence." Raoul had a shaved head and deep brown eyes. He stood up. "I really hope I don't become an Amanda Knox, or that guy in *The Shawshank Redemption*."

"We're going to do our best," Michel said.

"Yes," Clémence added. "You'll be out of here in no time. I have a good lead as to who the real murderer is."

Michel looked at her in surprise. "You do? Do the police know?"

"I just need to gather more evidence," said Clémence. "I'll tell them if I find out anything more." She turned back to Raoul. "Now I'm here to find out what you know. What's this I hear about you getting into a fight with Dupont on the street?"

Raoul sighed. "The guy was a jerk. I'm sorry that he died and everything. I just mean that he really was a jerk. Every time he came in to the store, he'd sneer at me. I didn't know why until I saw him on the street over a week ago. He called me racist names."

"What did he say?" Clémence asked.

Raoul was of Portuguese descent. His skin was the color of dark caramel. He told her the offending word, and Clémence nodded in sympathy.

"I had just been taking a smoke break from work and walking around the neighborhood. He brushed past me and insulted me for no good reason. Of course I got mad and confronted him. It was a very public blowup, and I ended up punching him in the eye. I regret it now, of course. It was a very stupid thing to do, but my anger got the best of me."

"And what did the police say when you told them that?"

"Well, they're using it against me. They seem to think this is more reason to think I'm guilty."

"This Dupont guy sounds like a piece of work," said Clémence. "I can see why somebody would want to kill him."

"He's a jerk, through and through."

"I just hope you don't say this if you're ever on trial," Michel warned. "It doesn't look good. You had been on the receiving end of his abuse and reacted in the heat of the moment. Poisoned éclairs are premeditated. However, they have no evidence that you had anything to do with them."

"So you're saying I have a good chance of being let go?"

Michel nodded. "Unless, of course, they find something else against you."

"So what do you know about Dupont?" Clémence asked both Michel and Raoul.

"Nothing," said Raoul. "Except he would come in and buy pastries all the time."

"He worked at a PR company and lived not far from Place d'Iena," said Michel.

"So he lived and worked near Damour," Clémence mused. "When he ate those éclairs, he was probably taking a lunch break, taking a long walk around the park." She turned to Michel again. "Can you give me the address of both his workplace and home?"

"I don't know," Michel said slowly. "That information is confidential."

"You can trust her," said Raoul. "She helped

the police solve a murder last month. She's good. Faster than the police, at least. I really don't know what these guys get paid for."

He launched into how she had found the person who killed la gardienne.

Michel looked at Clémence more closely. "What are you going to do with this information?"

"Nothing yet," said Clémence. "I'm just trying to match some details together with the suspect I have in mind."

Michel relented, nodding. "Okay. But don't say where you got the information. Dupont was married with no kids. He was quite wealthy."

"So he leaves a widow," said Clémence.

"Her name is Florence. She's a housewife, and she's probably making the funeral arrangements. Are you going to talk to her?"

Clémence nodded. "I will as soon as I get some things settled. Thanks for the info."

CHAPTER THIRTEEN

$\mathscr{A}$ t work the next morning, while in the kitchen, Sebastien and Berenice wanted the scoop on the investigation.

After Clémence filled them in, Celine came in. The *salon de thé* had not opened yet, and she had just changed into her uniform to start her shift.

"Who was that guy who was calling your name in the patisserie yesterday morning?" Celine asked. "I didn't know you were dating anyone."

Berenice perked up. Even Sebastien looked up from his tray of salmon éclairs.

"Arthur?" Clémence said. "We're not dating. He just lives in my building."

"Really? He's pretty hot."

"How hot?" Berenice said.

"He's tall, dark hair—"

"Oh come on," Clémence groaned. "He's this obnoxious neighbor I keep running into. He's the one I found the dead body with at the park when we were walking our dogs."

"Why don't you introduce him to us?" Celine grinned.

"Didn't I just say he's obnoxious?" Clémence replied. "Besides, you guys wouldn't like him. He's totally bourgeois, totally spoiled."

"Yeah, but Celine says he's gorgeous." Berenice teased.

"You both are already dating great guys," Clémence said.

Celine finally seemed to be getting over her crush on Sebastien now that she was dating Sam. At least, she seemed comfortable enough gossiping about other boys in front of him. Berenice was happily dating Ben.

"Seriously," Sebastien said. "You're three intelligent women. Don't you ever talk about anything besides boys?"

Berenice shot her brother a dirty look. "There's nothing wrong with that. It doesn't make us any less intelligent."

"Yes, but you're so obsessive."

"Don't tell me that you don't talk about girls with your guy friends," said Celine.

"We talk about other things, too," said Sebastien.

"Like what?" Berenice asked.

"Politics, sports, stuff that matter."

"We do talk about other things," said Celine.

"But it's more fun to talk about hot guys around you," said Berenice.

Clémence tried to be more diplomatic. "I get what you're saying, Seb, but love is the driving force for women. We're more connected with our emotions than you men are, and we love to be in love. Sure, we get obsessed about it, but it gives us a rush."

Sebastien shook his head. "Fine, whatever. In general, I think girls talk too much."

He turned back to his éclairs.

Celine looked at her watch. "I've got to start my shift."

"Speaking of love," Clémence said to Berenice. "How are things going with Ben, anyway? Has he kissed you yet?"

Berenice grinned and nodded. "He's a good kisser."

Sebastien groaned. He put on his iPod.

Clémence and Berenice laughed.

"We're exclusive now," said Berenice.

"That's great! Ben's one of the nicest guys I know."

"Although I do find his novel a bit strange. He's a super talented poet though. What about this Arthur guy? Why do you hate him so much?"

"I don't hate him," Clémence said. "He just gets on my nerves. He can say the rudest things, so I never know when he's going to turn into a jerk."

"You know," Berenice said slyly. "Some great love stories begin with two people hating each other."

"Ugh, come on. Arthur's a total playboy. He takes a different girl home every week."

"How do you know that?"

Clémence gave her a look. "He lives in my building. I know these things. Trust me. He's not the guy for me."

"All right. It just seems to me that you have a hard time finding guys who meet your standards. Maybe your standards are too high."

"On the contrary. I think they are way too low."

She told her about how she had accidentally gotten herself into a date with John Christopher, the murder suspect.

"No way!" Berenice exclaimed. She poked Sebastien on the arm.

"What?" Sebastien pulled down his earbuds, annoyed.

"Clémence is going on a date with the guy who might've poisoned Dupont."

Sebastien raised an eyebrow at Clémence.

"It's not a real date!" Clémence protested. "I'm just gathering information."

"Where are you going?" asked Berenice.

"I don't know yet. He's going to let me know. Actually, I haven't checked my phone all morning."

Clémence reached into her purse. There was indeed a new text message from John. "He wants to have dinner at La Coquette."

La Coquette was a chic restaurant not far from Damour at Place de Trocadéro.

"We'll go there too," Sebastien offered. "You can't go on a date with a murderer without backup."

"He's right," said Berenice. "For once. We'll just sit at a nearby table and listen in."

"I'll be recording the conversation on my phone," said Clémence. "I'm nervous about tonight."

"Don't be," said Berenice. "What are you going to wear?"

"Yes," Sebastien rolled his eyes, "because that's the most pressing matter Clémence has to deal with."

"Actually it is important," said Berenice. "The right outfit can make him talk even more. Dress to kill. Not literally, of course."

"I don't have anything too sexy."

"I'll come over to your house with a couple of dresses. I'm meeting Ben, anyway."

"Okay, great."

"I have this red dress I bought recently that I think you'll look good in. I even have a red lipstick to match it exactly."

"Red?" Clémence was unsure. She usually wore black, white, beige—classic neutrals that Parisian girls gravitated toward. She wasn't the type to like to draw too much attention to herself in a hyper-sexual way.

"Yes, get out of your comfort zone," said Berenice. "Remember, you're dressing sexy to save Raoul's life."

Sebastien groaned even louder. "Oh, please."

CHAPTER FOURTEEN

*C*lémence couldn't recognize herself in the mirror. With black cat eyeliner, loads of mascara, and the red lipstick to match the very tight and very short red dress, she looked like…a tart. three fifteen p.m., Clémence went to the 8th arrondissement where Christie's was located. She was on time for the nineteenth-century European painting auction.

"Va voom," said Berenice. "You're the hottest detective I've ever seen."

"I'm extremely uncomfortable," said Clémence. "Can I even sit down without my underwear showing?"

She walked over to the chair and sat down. It was very risky. She would have to cross her legs the entire evening. Luckily the restaurant was only a five-minute walk from her house. She had told John that she would meet him there.

Berenice was already in her outfit for dinner, which was a much less revealing, modest black dress so that she and Sebastien could stay incognito.

Clémence put on black pumps. Although she knew how to walk in four-inch heels, she didn't do it often, and she stumbled a bit. Berenice made her walk a bit for practice.

"Sashay your hips more when you do," she said.

"Is all this really necessary?" Clémence said. "It's a date, not prostitution."

"Don't worry. You won't look out of place at that restaurant. It's full of millionaires with their model girlfriends."

"True."

"So let's go."

John was already waiting for her when she went inside the restaurant. She remembered to maintain an erect posture to display confidence. His eyes widened when he saw her. He was in what looked like his best Italian tux, with a pink handkerchief to match his silk pink tie.

He pulled out her chair for her at the table. She looked around the chic pink and black decorated restaurant. Fancy people, fancy food. There was even a waterfall on one wall.

Aside from Damour, she hadn't dined in an expensive restaurant for a long time. During her travels, she preferred street food, unless her family came to visit her. Since she had been back in Paris, she hadn't been on dinner dates at all. Instead, she'd go out with her friends to bars, especially in the less posh neighborhoods, where all the young people gathered.

It felt nice in a way to be on a nice date, even if there was a high chance that John was some sort of psychopathic killer. She looked at him, but he seemed a bit nervous when he smiled at her.

Nervous? Why would he be nervous? But perhaps it was because despite his education and self-made wealth, he'd grown up in a more humble environment. Clémence could relate to that. She hadn't grown up in the 16th herself, and she never had really gotten used to mingling with the bourgeoisie. It took her a while to learn which wine went with what, which forks to use, and what the items on the menus even were.

The waiter came by with the menus and announced the specialties of the day.

"What will you have?" John asked.

"Um, perhaps the lobster pasta," Clémence said. She'd been so nervous about the date that she'd lost her appetite, but now that she was here, she realized she hadn't really eaten lunch and the hunger descended. "What about you?"

"The same," he said.

After they ordered, they chatted about his work. He had been excited about the transfer, as he had learned French in school growing up and it had gotten a bit rusty.

"It's been hard to get to know my French colleagues," he said, sipping his glass of Moët champagne. "But they seem to be coming around."

"Yes, the French are a bit harder to pry open," said Clémence. "But once you're in, you're in."

"I hope I'm in with you," John looked at her in a sexy way. Under the dimness of the lights, his green eyes didn't look cold at all, as Marie had claimed, especially when he smiled at her that way.

"We'll see about that," Clémence teased.

"So what do you do, Anabelle?"

Oh, right. Clémence had almost forgotten that her name was supposed to be Anabelle Bernard.

"I work in public relations," she said. "At JJ Anders. Have you heard of it?"

John shook his head. "I haven't, unfortunately."

"What about Preston & Olivier? They're our biggest competitor."

Preston & Olivier was the name of the PR company Dupont worked for, where he was *directeur de l'agence*.

"Oh, yes," said John. "It sounds familiar. Actually, I think I have a neighbor who works there."

Clémence perked up. "Who?"

"I know his last name is Dupont, from the name on his buzzer. But I can't remember his first name."

"Is it Alexandre Dupont?" Clémence helped. "He's the boss at Preston & Olivier."

"Yes, that sounds right," said John. "He mentioned working there. We had a nice chat in the courtyard. I guess he wanted to practice a bit of English."

"When was the last time you talked to him?" asked Clémence.

"Early this week?" he said. "He gave me all sorts of recommendations for stores and restaurants this neighborhood. He's a man who loves to eat."

Clémence frowned. "So you don't know?"

"Don't know what?"

"Dupont is dead."

She looked closely at his face. His expression twisted into shock.

"Dead? What do you mean?"

"You really didn't know?"

"No," he exclaimed. "How?"

"I don't know," Clémence lied. "Our company just received word that he'd passed last Thursday. It was also in the papers. He was poisoned."

"What?"

Either John was a skilled actor or he was genuinely shocked. Weren't sociopaths good at acting?

"Yes," said Clémence. "By pistachio éclairs. The police are investigating who would poison him."

"Oh, God," said John. "That's shocking. I was just talking to him a few days ago. I didn't know. I've seen his wife lately, but she was always in a rush and didn't seem as friendly as she usually is. Now I know why. But pistachio éclairs—were they from Damour?"

"Yes. Why?"

"Because he had been talking about them, saying how they were just the best things ever created. He talked about them in so much detail that the next morning I rushed out to the patisserie and bought two of them before work." John gave a nervous laugh. "I'm glad they weren't poisoned. It's strange, isn't it? I wonder who would be out to get him?"

"He is a formidable man in the workplace," said Clémence.

"Yes, it could be someone from work. Or one of his competitors."

Clémence nodded. John could be right.

She was disappointed that John didn't seem to be involved in the murder, although she did find out that he was connected to Dupont. This could be useful.

At least she wasn't on a date with a dangerous killer, after all. Even if she was lying about her identity, it was a date, and she hadn't been on one of those in a while.

They enjoyed the rest of their evening peacefully. Their food was delicious, and John continued to be an attentive date. She knew that Berenice and Sebastien were seated a table away, but at one point she turned to them and quickly smiled to indicate that everything was okay.

John was superficially attractive in the conventional sense, but she didn't know whether they had much in common. The conversation flowed easily enough, however, and at one point Clémence thought she wouldn't mind seeing John again.

After they finished their coffee at the end of the meal, Clémence said she'd better be heading home. They got up after John paid, and Clémence had trouble once again with her balance in her four-inch heels after sitting down for more than two hours. She stumbled a bit and lightly bumped into someone.

"Clémence?"

It was Arthur. Standing behind him was a hot blonde wearing a silver minidress even shorter than her red dress.

John looked between Clémence and Arthur, confused.

Clémence shot Arthur a look. "You must be mistaken. *Je m'appelle Anabelle.*"

John stepped in and introduced himself to Arthur. "How do you know Anabelle?"

"We're neighbors," Clémence said.

"Yes," Arthur said slowly. "Just up the street."

"Up the street?" John looked at Clémence again. "I thought you said you lived in the 8th."

"I—I do," Clémence lied. "But my parents live here."

She looked at the blonde, and a feeling grew in the pit of her stomach. The girl had the poutiest red lips. She could've been a model if she had fewer curves. Clémence felt the food in her stomach churning.

"This is Lea," said Arthur.

John was looking at her too, but trying not to. Lea smiled and thrusted her chest out even more. Arthur, however, gave Clémence a quick once-over. Clémence felt embarrassed. She must've looked so odd trying to dress up like one of the sexy girls.

"We'll leave you to your dinner," said Clémence, turning away. *"Bonne soirée."*

She followed John out the door.

"Who was that?" asked John.

"Oh," said Clémence. She quickly tried to come up with something. "We dated once, but he must've not remembered my name."

"That was weird," said John. "He seemed sure your name was Clémence."

"He's just a jerk," said Clémence. "He probably forgets the names of all the girls he dates."

"I don't think he will forget the name of the girl he's with tonight," John joked.

Clémence nodded and forced a smile. She wondered if John was the bigger jerk to comment on the sexiness of another girl while he was on a date with her. She couldn't wait to go home.

"I don't live far from here," said John. "Do you want to come over and have coffee?"

"But we just had coffee," said Clémence. Then she realized what he was suggesting. "Oh. No. I really have to get home."

She flagged down a cab, to continue on with the charade of living in the 8th.

"Well I had a great time," said John. "I'll call you."

"Sure." Clémence smiled weakly. She kissed him good-bye on both cheeks. She didn't have it in her to keep up the pretense of enthusiasm anymore.

She got into the cab. She asked the cabbie to drive around the block once and then drop her off at 14 Avenue Kléber.

She was furious with Arthur. He had almost blown her cover.

That was what she was mad at him for, wasn't it?

CHAPTER FIFTEEN

"We saw the whole thing," Berenice said the next morning in the kitchen. "Although we couldn't hear much over the conversations in that restaurant."

Clémence wasn't feeling so well. She couldn't sleep the night before. She had kept thinking about the blond bombshell that Arthur had taken out to dinner. How foolish she'd felt when her own date had drooled over Lea.

Was she jealous because John had taken an interest in the blonde or because Arthur was going out with her? She didn't think she cared what Arthur did, but when she got home from the date, she couldn't sleep. She kept imagining Arthur bringing his date back up to his little room on the top floor.

"What an evening," Clémence said, sighing.

"But you looked like you were having a good time," said Berenice. "So we gather that this guy is not the killer, after all?"

"No. But he is Dupont's neighbor." She explained how Dupont had recommended the pistachio éclairs to John, and that had been why he bought them.

"Weird coincidence," said Sebastien.

Clémence nodded. "John bought two because he was going to give one to a colleague, but it was so good that he ended up eating both of them."

"If that's not a testimony to my baking powers, I don't know what is." Sebastien crossed his arms and looked proud.

"But I've hit a wall," said Clémence. "I was really hoping it was John. Now I'll have to look into Dupont's enemies, although that's what the inspector's doing. How am I supposed to infiltrate his company? Poor Raoul. I just feel so responsible."

"It's really not your fault." Sebastien's voice was full of kindness and Clémence appreciated it

Lately she'd been too overwhelmed by everything and felt extremely frustrated.

"Ça va aller," Sebastien continued. "It's going to be all right. Raoul didn't do it, and they're going to figure it out, sooner or later. You're not responsible for this man's death. He just happened to love the éclairs so much that somebody took advantage of that. You don't have to do anything. It's the police's job to catch the murderer anyway. Just relax."

Clémence felt soothed by his words. There was something incredibly calming about Sebastien, and she felt better already.

"You're right." She blinked back the tears that were on the verge of forming.

"No need to fret," said Berenice. "You know your hot neighbor last night?"

"Arthur?" Clémence made a face.

"Did you see his face when he saw you in your dress?" Berenice said. "He couldn't stop staring at you."

"You did look pretty good," Sebastien admitted.

"Well, my date was drooling over *his* date," said Clémence.

"We left shortly after you did, but Arthur was staring at you the whole time you walked toward the door. I was surprised he didn't run after you."

Clémence waved her comments away. "There's no way. Arthur does not care one bit about me."

"Didn't you say he had coffee with you when you waited for John to appear outside the bank?"

"Yeah, but he doesn't have much going on with his life. Apparently, he's working on his PhD, but he seems to be going about it in a leisurely way. I see him going to the tennis court all the time."

Berenice gave her a look. "How can you miss the signs? He's into you. And it sounds like you've been spending a lot of time together recently."

"It's just a coincidence. He lives in the same building, and we're bound to run into each other."

"I'm telling you," Berenice said. "He's into you."

"Stop," Clémence said. She was starting to get annoyed. Now she knew how Sebastien felt when Berenice bugged him about his love life. "Arthur would stare at anything in a tight dress. There's nothing going on between us." She took off her apron. "I think I need to take a personal day."

Sebastien looked at her in sympathy. Berenice started to apologize, but Clémence shook her head.

"No, don't apologize. I'm just stressed out, and I need a break to relax. I've been working every day this week, so I should just go chill out."

CHAPTER SIXTEEN

*C*lémence took a long walk along the river. She looked into the glimmering waters of La Seine as she headed toward Palais de Tokyo. The skateboarders were out in front of the huge museum, doing tricks near the fountain. People sitting in the museum's outdoor café were chatting, laughing, and having a good time. Watching them, she felt a bit lonely.

She turned back to look at her old friend, *la Tour Eiffel*. There were a million things on her mind. She hoped the tower would give her guidance.

Maybe she wasn't so good at solving murder cases, after all. The first one had just been luck— the victim had been someone in her building, and it was a lot easier to interrogate people. With this

Dupont guy, it was probably best to let the police
handle it. She would just have to pray that Raoul
would be let go soon. She hoped that Cyril had
some other leads and was not just putting all his
energy into finding more evidence against Raoul.

Clémence wished she could do more, but she
felt foolish enough going undercover as some cheap
date. She was lucky that no one she knew had seen
her. No one except Arthur, that was.

Arthur. The thought of him made her blush all
over again. She had to admit it to herself: she was
attracted to him. But she couldn't understand why.
He came from the worst kind of upper-class fami-
lies and he slept around, plus he wore pink dress
shirts and cashmere sweaters tied around his shoulders. Personality-wise, he was as abrasive as a
cactus, he was a snob, and he was arrogant.

But he was also handsome, educated, and rich.
Even Clémence had to admit that he was a catch
for many girls; it was obvious why he had such an
easy time finding girls to sleep with. She chided
herself for liking a guy with such shallow taste in
women. Then again, Arthur must've liked this Lea
girl, if he would take her to such a good restaurant.

Clémence sighed. Arthur could also be kind
sometimes. He liked dogs and was good with them.

As far as she could tell, he was a good brother to his siblings. And he was doing something with his life, even though he was taking his sweet time with it. She had to admit he was reliable, since he was there when she needed help.

Maybe that was why she liked him: he had the potential to be a good guy. However, she couldn't like someone because of misguided hope. She'd had one too many bad experiences to know that she couldn't accept Arthur as he was, right now.

As she looked at la tour, she said a little prayer, asking to help her get over this little crush on Arthur. For good measure, she also prayed for this murder case to be solved, if not by her, then by the police.

Near Place d'Iéna, she turned back home. She enjoyed the rest of the walk along the Seine. People jogged, biked, or rollerbladed past her, and she felt as if everybody was happy to be in the sunshine. The sun had made a grand appearance after a cloudy morning. It put her in a good mood as she walked back up to the Palais de Chaillot.

As she made her way to the roundabout at Place du Trocadéro, a sight of a boy on a scooter caught her eye. He wore a blue helmet with a familiar frog on it. He was turning down Avenue Raymond Poincaré.

He could have been the same boy who had bought the two pistachio éclairs from her store. Even though he was only about eleven years old, there was no harm in asking him about it, so she did.

"Bonjour, excusez-moi!" She chased after the little boy.

He didn't hear her and continued on his merry way. Clémence was wearing flats, so she was able to run and catch up to him.

The boy stopped when she blocked his path, looking wide-eyed at her. Clémence smiled to put him at ease. She explained that she worked at the Damour patisserie, and she'd seen him in there buying their products. She then lied and said that she was doing a survey on customer satisfaction and if he'd been willing to participate.

The boy nodded and asked if that meant he got a free treat from the store. Clémence laughed, surprised by his boldness.

"Sure, how about an éclair?" Clémence said.

"I don't like éclairs as much as *pains au chocolat*," he said.

"You don't? But didn't I see you buying two pistachio éclairs this week?"

"Oh, that wasn't for me," the boy said. "That was for someone else."

"Who?"

"I don't know. A lady asked me to buy them for her and said that she'd give me five euros if I did."

"Why?"

The boy shrugged. "I guess she didn't want to wait in line. She said to meet her around the corner when I was done."

"What did she look like?"

He thought about it. "She was wearing sunglasses, and had blond hair."

"So you don't know who she is?" she pressed.

"No."

"How long was her hair?"

"Maybe here." He put his hands to his collar-bone to show the length.

"So this is not a lady that your mother would know?"

"No. She's a stranger."

"Didn't your mother ever tell you not to talk to strangers?" Clémence said, even though she was a stranger herself.

"She's a lady," said the boy. "Ladies aren't dangerous."

Or are they? Clémence thought.

"What was she wearing?" she asked.

"I think a black coat," he said. "But I don't remember. Can I get my *pain au chocolat* now?"

"Sure," Clémence said. "Let's go to the patisserie."

This woman, whoever she was, must've wanted to be in disguise. Although it had been sunny that morning. Maybe the weather had warranted sunglasses.

The woman must've planned the poisoning. She hadn't wanted to be seen buying the pistachio éclairs herself, so she hired a boy off the street to do it.

Whoever it was must've known that Dupont liked his pistachio éclairs. And by the sound of it, he had told whomever he ran into how much he liked them. This blond lady was the key. She might just be the murderer!

CHAPTER SEVENTEEN

"Who could this woman be?" Clémence asked Berenice in the employee lounge.

"What about the wife?" asked Berenice.

"I thought about her, but I saw a picture of Dupont and his wife on the Internet where they were at some fancy event, and the wife has short brunette hair. In any case, I should weasel a meeting with her."

Berenice nodded. "For sure, but what are you going to say?"

"It's awkward, isn't it? Maybe she wouldn't want to talk to just any girl off the street. I'm not a real inspector, and I can't impersonate one. Otherwise Cyril will have a reason to lock me up."

"Okay, what about John? You can get him to introduce you."

Clémence groaned. "Haven't I been through enough? He didn't even text me."

She checked her phone to prove it. To her surprise, there was a text from John.

Coucou beautiful, it was fun last night. Do you want to have drinks tomorrow?

"Tomorrow," Berenice said. "He wants to see you again so soon. He must like you."

"I can't continue on with this charade however. I have to tell him who I really am."

"You will?"

"Yes," said Clémence. "He has a good sense of humor. I hope he'll understand that I had to do what I had to do."

"And if he doesn't?"

"I don't know, but he's bound to find out sooner or later. He works at the bank in this neighborhood, so there's a high chance of running into him. I can't pretend to be Anabelle forever."

"True," said Berenice. "And sometimes your pictures are in the gossip column for being the heiress of Damour. Why did you stop going to events, anyway?"

"I used to do that with Mathieu," said

Clémence. "He liked going to those fancy parties and making important connections. I was never into the whole socialite scene."

"Too bad," said Berenice. "I think it would be cool to have a famous friend."

"I'd want to be famous for my accomplishments, not what my parents have achieved," said Clémence.

Which reminded her that as soon as this murder case was solved, she could go back to her art. This thought prompted her to contact John right away. She wanted the case to be closed as soon as possible.

Can we meet? she texted him.

At the café across the street from the bank, Clémence explained everything.

John was shocked at first, but then his expression slowly melted into understanding.

"So you used me," he said.

"I'm so sorry," said Clémence. "I had to be careful because I thought you were a killer."

"Wow." He laughed incredulously.

"I didn't know you then."

"So were you ever interested in me at all?"

Clémence hesitated. "Well, sure. I thought we had a good time. We had some good conversations, and you're an attractive guy."

"Just attractive?"

"Beau," she said, smiling. *"Comme un dieu."*

He smiled back. "Okay, flattery will get you everywhere."

"Do you think that you can help me in any way?"

He rubbed his chin. "I was shocked after you told me that Dupont died. I can understand what you're trying to do. You're right. The police are useless here. When I got pickpocketed on the Métro the first week I was here, the police basically laughed at me and told me it was useless to get my wallet back."

Clémence nodded knowingly. "Like I said, they've arrested my employee, and he's innocent. I guess I can tell the police about what I found out so far, but I want to speak to the wife first. She would be privy to the secrets of her husband."

"Unless this blonde is his mistress. Or what if the wife is the killer? Imagine, my own neighbor, a killer."

"That's why I want to find out in a non-interrogative way, but I can't seem to find out anything about this wife online."

"Well I can pay Madame Dupont a casual visit. She's quite elusive, and I don't see much of her, but Dupont's funeral should be soon, and I can try to get an invite."

"That would be great," she said. "So you haven't talked to her in the past?"

"I only run into her when she's out doing the shopping, and we exchange friendly hellos." John frowned, thinking of something. "I do remember that once I was meditating in the living room, and I heard them arguing."

"Arguing?"

"Well, it was just Dupont doing the yelling. Maybe he'd been arguing with someone on the phone."

"Did he do that any other times?"

John nodded. "A few occasions, yes, but then again, I only moved in there three weeks ago, and I'm usually at work or out exploring the city, so I'm not home all the time to know what's going on. It does sound like Dupont has a temper."

"I wonder who he was arguing with," said Clémence.

"I guess we'll find out, hopefully. After work, I'll

pay Madame Dupont a visit, and I'll let you know what happens."

"Great," said Clémence.

"And hopefully you can be my date to this funeral."

"It's a date, then."

"And if you do solve this case with my help, you owe me dinner, this time."

Clémence looked at John, who was grinning in a teasing way.

"Fine," she said. "I guess it's only fair."

CHAPTER EIGHTEEN

The lawyers were helping Raoul build up his defense, but even Clémence's parents were worried that it had gotten to this point. Michel and the other lawyers had shown the police the security footage obtained from the store, arguing that there was no proof that Raoul tampered with the éclairs in any way. However, it also proved that Dupont didn't even buy the éclairs. They could argue that Raoul had given Dupont the éclairs outside of the store.

Clémence was concerned for Raoul, as well. She hoped that John would come through with something. He had a charm that she was sure most women wouldn't be able to resist. Sure enough,

while she was eating dinner, he called to say that
there was a funeral tomorrow.

"How did Madame Dupont act when you
talked to her?" Clémence asked.

"She looked pretty tired," said John. "I guess
she's still distraught. Wouldn't blame her really.
Her eyes were red, so she had probably been
crying. She seemed really embarrassed to have me
see her in that state so I kept the conversation
short. She told me about the funeral, and that
was it."

After noting down the details, Clémence made
plans to meet with John.

"If you wear a black version of the dress you
wore on our last date, I'll be happy," he said.

"There's zero chance of that happening," said
Clémence. "But I will wear black, if that pleases
you."

"That pleases the dead. I'm sure you'll look hot
in anything."

"Thank you."

Clémence hung up, a small smile still on her
lips. John was wrong for her. She knew it, but she
still enjoyed flirting with him.

As she turned off the lights in the kitchen to go
into her bedroom to retire for the evening, her

doorbell rang. Who could it be at this hour? She looked through the peephole.

Arthur.

"Yes?" She opened the door a crack.

He was in a gray V-neck T-shirt and jeans. He was dressed casually and he looked quite good.

"The new *gardien* mixed up some of our mail," he said.

Since *la gardienne*, the caretaker of their building, had been murdered last month, they got a new caretaker, an older man in his late fifties. The mixed mail wasn't a surprise, but what did surprise her was that Arthur came himself.

She raised an eyebrow. "Shouldn't one of your many maids be doing these kinds of errands?"

Arthur shrugged, stone-faced. "I might as well, since I know you. Plus I wanted an update as to how you were doing with this murder case."

"Everything's going well," Clémence said.

She took the letters from Arthur's hand. It was just a couple of bills for her parents.

"You need any help with it?"

"The case? No, I got it. You almost messed up my investigation, by the way."

"Right, I realized that after. So that was the banker guy you had been stalking?"

"My lead, yes."

"And your investigation required you to date?"

Clémence could feel her defensive wall going up.

"Yes, Arthur," she said sarcastically. "If you're going to call me a whore, go ahead."

His eyes widened. "I wasn't going to call you a whore. I was just surprised to see you dressed that way, that's all."

"Why? The girls you go out with dress like that. How is Lea, by the way?"

"We're not going out," Arthur said quickly. "She's just a friend."

"Sure. Anyway, thanks for stopping by."

"*Attends.*" Arthur put a hand on the door. "Wait. This banker guy—"

"John," said Clémence.

"John, whatever. Are you sure you're safe around him?"

"Yes, he's helping me. I only see him in public places, anyway."

"You're not going out with him again, are you?"

"If a funeral counts," Clémence said, and then immediately regretted it. She didn't want Arthur to get into her business again. "Look, he's not the murderer, and I've already revealed my identity to him. He's Dupont's neighbor, and he's going to help me get to know the wife."

She quickly explained what she'd found out about John.

"So you think the wife did it?" Arthur asked.

"I don't know. I'm trying to find out."

"Well, it's clear that you don't know much at this point. This banker guy can still be a suspect. Remember when you almost got killed last time when you were left alone with someone you thought you could trust?"

It was true that Clémence had placed herself in a dangerous situation last month, but she had learned from it, and she was smarter this time.

"It's going to be fine," she said, although doubts were forming. Arthur did find her unconscious last time, and he even went to the hospital with her.

"Like I said, I'm willing to be your bodyguard. Just tell me where you're going to be, and I'll show up discreetly and watch your back."

Clémence thought about it. She guessed it would be practical to have help in case anything went wrong.

"Fine," she said.

"I'll give you my number," said Arthur, then pulled out his phone to take hers.

After they exchanged numbers, he left.

Clémence closed the doors and sighed. Spending more time with Arthur wasn't going to help her get over him. Even though he claimed that Lea was just a friend, nobody wanted to be "just friends" with a blond bombshell. She was sure he was sleeping around, and she wasn't going to be another notch on his belt.

She would just accept his help in this case, and that would be it.

CHAPTER NINETEEN

*P*aris was raining, a fitting day for a funeral. While Dupont's burial was reserved for family and close friends, John had been invited to a restaurant next to the cemetery reserved for Dupont's party to pay his respects.

Clémence met John in front of the restaurant. He looked handsome in his black suit. She wore a long, demure black dress with black tights and flats.

They peeked inside the windows. The place was full of people. She spotted Madame Dupont chatting with a couple of people in a corner. They went in. She looked around for any blond women at the party, and she spotted two. One was a bottled blonde in her forties. Her hair was cut to her chin.

Another woman was younger, in her late twenties or early thirties, with wavy hair up to her chest. The little boy did say that the woman who paid him to buy the éclairs had long blond hair.

She texted Arthur a description of the woman, asking him to chat her up. Arthur was already there. His cover was a former employee at Dupont's company.

"Who are you texting?" John asked.

"Just a friend," Clémence said.

"Come on. Let me introduce you to Madame Dupont."

"Okay."

As the others paid their respects, Clémence waited for her turn. Madame Florence Dupont was a short, small-boned woman with sunken cheeks and gray-blue eyes.

"This is my girlfriend Anabelle," John said after Madame Dupont greeted him.

"I'm so sorry for your loss," Clémence said.

"Thank you," she replied. "I don't know why anybody would do this to my sweet husband."

Tears dripped from her eyes, which she quickly wiped away with a white handkerchief.

"It's tragic." Clémence tried to tread softly.

"Your husband sounded like he had a powerful position. Could it have been one of his competitors?"

"Maybe. But I heard from the police that they've already arrested someone."

"Who?" asked Clémence, even though she already knew.

"Somebody who works at a patisserie. Apparently my husband had a spat with this guy."

"What about?"

"Oh, I don't know, Alex did have a temper sometimes. Maybe he went over the edge. His anger was his weakness, I suppose."

"Well, nobody's perfect," said Clémence. "And he didn't deserve to be killed this way."

"No."

"Did he have any enemies at work?"

"I don't know," said Madame Dupont. "Not as far as I know. I don't know much about his work life except when I go to holiday parties, although I guess it could be someone from his work. He could be bossy with people. He was very demanding. But I still loved him."

After exchanging a few more words, Clémence conversed with John about the exchange.

"She seems to be sincere," said Clémence.

John nodded. "She is crying a lot."

Clémence frowned. "It's disappointing that she doesn't know anything."

She checked her phone. Arthur hadn't texted her back, but she saw him chatting with the blonde in a corner.

Arthur's body language was open—too open. He had a hand on the girl's elbow, and he was looking down at her, nodding sympathetically. Clémence's face burned. She hoped he wasn't going to try to pick her up.

When the blonde took a phone call and moved away, she told John that she was going to the washroom. There, she called Arthur.

"*Alors?* Well?"

"She works at Dupont's company," said Arthur. "Her name is Lydia Baudet. She seems upset, but not upset enough. Many of his coworkers are here out of obligation. It doesn't sound like Dupont was well-liked, but rather well-respected."

"How do we get more information out of her?"

"Do you want me to ask her out on a date?"

"Oh, you'd like that, wouldn't you?"

"Are you jealous?" Arthur teased.

"Please. If you think you can get more out of

her, be my guest and take her out. Just don't come crying when she poisons you."

"It's only fair. You went on a fake date with a potential murderer, so now I get to."

Clémence hung up. If she could admit it to herself, she didn't want Arthur going out with the murderous blonde. She was just his type, except for the murderous part. If only she could just find out more about her on her own. Perhaps she could ask Madame Dupont what she knew about this Lydia Baudet.

Clémence came out of the restroom and looked around for Madame Dupont. She noticed her walking up to the second floor of the restaurant with an old lady. She hadn't paid much attention to the lady until now. She was tiny, with powder white hair. Clémence followed them. Perhaps it would be nice to be able to talk to her in private after she spoke with the elderly lady.

When Clémence reached upstairs, she realized this floor was empty. Madame Dupont and the lady were speaking softly, and Clémence tiptoed along the narrow hallway that led to a private room.

"How did you learn how to cry like that?" the old lady asked.

Madame Dupont gave a low, bitter chuckle. "As if I didn't cry enough living with that man."

"Well good riddance, darling. Now you'll get everything, and nobody suspects a thing. Well done, dear."

"Yes, Mother. We'll be able to live in peace."

Clémence took out her smartphone to record the conversation. Unfortunately, just after she pressed record, her phone began to ring.

It was Arthur! Again!

"Shit," she muttered.

"Someone's out there," the elderly lady said.

Madame Dupont and her mother poked their heads out to the hallway. Clémence hid her phone up her sleeve, hoping Arthur was listening on the other end.

"What are you doing here?" Madame Dupont asked.

"I was trying to find les toilettes?" Clémence said innocently, looking around and trying to act clueless.

But Madame Dupont wasn't buying it. She narrowed her eyes at her. "How much did you hear?"

"Who is this?" the elderly woman asked.

"I don't know," Madame Dupont looked at

Clémence sharply. "I should've known you were some sort of snoop, asking all those questions earlier."

She was furious, but they were at a public event. Madame Dupont was cornered, and she looked a bit frightened.

"I work at Damour," said Clémence. "So it was you! You were the one who hired a boy off the street to buy pistachio éclairs. Then you poisoned the éclairs."

"I don't know what you're talking about." She feigned ignorance.

"Come off it," said Clémence. "I heard everything. You wore a blond wig when you hired the little boy, right? And I heard you talking about how you were fake crying tonight. About nobody suspecting a thing?"

"She was talking about something else," the elderly lady said lamely

"And you." Clémence turned to the old lady. "You should be ashamed of yourself, encouraging your daughter to murder her husband like that. Why?"

"All right," said Madame Dupont. "Fine. You want to know why? I'll tell you why. Dupont abused me for years. Like I said, his temper was his downfall. When I married him, I thought my life was like a fairy tale. This rich, handsome guy whisking me away, not caring about my lower middle-class background, but after a few months of marriage, he began beating me. Whenever he was frustrated with work, he'd beat me until I gathered into a ball, crying in a corner."

"It's true," said the elderly lady. "He deserved what he got. My girl has a huge bruise on her back, and scars all over her body."

"You see this face?" She pointed at herself. "Light bruises covered with heavy makeup. Sometimes I couldn't wear short-sleeved shirts and skirts because of my scars and bruises. I hated him. And I didn't want to go back to working in retail if I divorced him, so he got what he deserved."

"So you just poisoned your husband?" Clémence. "You couldn't just, you know, report that he's abusing you?"

"No. I could've, but why would I, when I could get the ultimate revenge and get everything? The apartment, the summerhouse in Greece, and his stakes in his company? And you, little snit—you're not going to ruin it for me."

Madame Dupont lunged at Clémence, who

screamed down to the lower floor for help. Arthur came running up with John behind him.

Arthur tore Madame Dupont away, and Clémence took out the phone from her sleeve.

"I have everything recorded," she said. "And now, I'm calling the police."

John held down Madame Dupont's trembling mother as Clémence called Cyril.

CHAPTER TWENTY

"She confessed on tape," Clémence said to Cyril. "You have to let Raoul go now."

Cyril's face was red, but he took a deep breath. "Fine. It would be wrong to detain the wrong man. I just don't know how you did it."

"Somebody had to find the right killer," she said. "And we both know it wasn't going to be you."

Clémence knew she shouldn't rub her good luck in Cyril's face, but she couldn't help it. It was too easy.

"Congratulations," he said sarcastically. "Come to the station."

"I'll be there in an hour," she said. "I want to enjoy the sunshine while it lasts."

Cyril fumed and stalked away. Madame Dupont

and her mother were handcuffed and escorted out of the restaurant.

Clémence went outside to get some air. Her heart had been beating wildly, but it had also been such a thrill. Now she needed to calm down again, take a walk around the block.

John followed her out the door. Arthur did too.

"That was amazing," said John.

"Are you okay?" Arthur asked her.

"I just need to get some air," said Clémence. But she grinned. "That was pretty cool wasn't it? We did it!"

John turned to Arthur. "I'm sorry, but who are you again?"

Arthur's face darkened as he met John's eyes. "We've met. We ran into you at the restaurant."

John slowly nodded. "Oh. Right. You were with a date. A blonde."

"Yes, but she wasn't a date. She was just a friend."

"Anyway, what were you doing here?"

"Clémence needed backup," Arthur said, his jaw clenching. "So she called me."

"Actually, I didn't call you," said Clémence. "You offered your help—"

"Why would Clémence need backup, when she

has me?" John asked, meeting Arthur's intense stare.

"Because we weren't sure who the killer was."

John turned back to Clémence. "Did you still think I was the killer?"

"No. Arthur is just cautious. You see, last month I was hurt when I was trying to solve a murder case, so he wanted to protect me this time."

"I hope both of you know by now that I'm not a murderer," said John.

"Yes, of course," said Clémence. "I'm sorry. Your help was invaluable. Wasn't it, Arthur?"

"Whatever," he said. "Come on, Clémence. Let's go home."

"I can walk my date home," John said.

"Clémence and I live in the same building," Arthur said. "So it's much more convenient if she walks with me."

"You do?" John said, startled.

Clémence didn't know what John was getting worked up about. She wasn't his girlfriend. And Arthur was acting strange, as well. He had wanted to go out with some murderous blonde just moments earlier.

"It's been a crazy day," said Clémence. "I think

I'm going to take a walk around the neighborhood —solo."

She turned on her heel, leaving the two guys with their jaws dropped.

Clémence did want to be alone. It had been not only a long day but also a very long and stressful week. Competition brought out the worst in men, and she didn't have the energy to deal with that. John and Arthur were handsome, but both men were wrong for her. There was no denying that she did have feelings for Arthur, but now that the case was solved, she hoped their lives wouldn't be as entangled and she would get over him.

She headed back to the Seine. She wanted to celebrate peacefully, and this included having a silent chat with la tour about her victory. She was proud of herself. Raoul would get out now, and she could finally go back to her routine of inventing new pastries with her bakers. She'd even have time to start painting again, since she was seriously considering Ben's offer of putting on a show.

For now, she was free, and she took in the beauty of the city in the springtime.

ÉCLAIR RECIPES

The popular French éclair pastry is made with choux dough. It is topped with icing or glazing, and the dough is filled with cream. The dough is typically oblong in shape. It's meant to be eaten in a few bites. To make different flavors of éclairs, start with the choux as a base.

Makes 9

Choux Recipe:
- 1/2 cup butter
- 1 cup all-purpose flour
- 1 cup water
- 4 eggs
- 1/4 teaspoon salt

Preheat oven to 450 degrees F (230 degrees C).

In a saucepan, combine water and butter and bring to a boil. Stir until the butter melts completely. Reduce the heat to low and add flour and salt. Stir vigorously until the mixture leaves the sides of the pan and begins to form a stiff ball.

Remove the pan from the heat. Add the eggs one at a time. Beat them in and incorporate completely.

Spoon or pour this mixture into a pastry bag with a large tip. Pipe onto a cookie sheet in 1 1/2 x 4 inch strips.

Bake for 15 minutes, then reduce heat to 325 degrees F (165 degrees C) and bake for 20 more minutes. They should be hollow sounding when you tap them lightly on the bottom. Cool completely on a wire rack.

Now that you know how to make the choux shells, you are open to experiment with different sweet and savory recipes by changing the fillings.

RECIPE 1: EASY CHOCOLATE ÉCLAIRS

Makes 9

Ingredients:

- Choux shells

Filling:

- 1 package (5 ounces) instant vanilla pudding mix
- 2 1/2 cups cold milk
- 1 cup heavy cream
- 1/4 cup confectioners' sugar
- 1 tsp vanilla

Combine pudding mix and milk in a medium bowl according to the package directions.

In a separate bowl, beat cream with an electric mixer until soft peaks form. Beat in sugar and vanilla. Fold whipped cream into pudding.

Cut the tops off the choux shells with a sharp knife. Fill the shells with pudding mixture and replace tops.

Icing:

- 2 (1 ounce) squares of semisweet chocolate
- 2 tbsp butter
- 1 cup confectioners' sugar
- 1 tsp vanilla
- 3 tbsp hot water

Melt the butter and chocolate in a medium saucepan over low heat. Stir in the sugar and vanilla. Stir in hot water, one tablespoon at a time, until icing is smooth and has reached desired consistency.

Remove from heat and cool slightly. Drizzle over filled éclairs (or dip the top of the shell in the icing). Refrigerate before serving—that is, if you can't resist biting into one right away!

RECIPE 2: PISTACHIO ÉCLAIRS

Makes 9

Ingredients:
- Choux shells
- Pistachio Pastry Cream
- 1 1/2 cups whole milk
- 4 large egg yolks
- 1/4 cup sugar
- 3 Tbsp cornstarch, sifted
- 1 jar (7 oz) Bonte Pistachio Cream

Fill a large bowl with ice cubes and water and set aside.

In a small saucepan, boil the milk and set aside.

In a medium saucepan, whisk together the egg

yolks, sugar, and cornstarch. While whisking, drizzle one quarter of the hot milk over the yolks. Continue adding the hot milk, half a cup at a time, until it has been incorporated. Put the pan over medium heat. Bring to a boil while whisking vigorously. Keep at the boil (still whisking) until thick (about 1 to 3 minutes), then take off the heat and whisk in the pistachio cream.

Scrape the mixture into a large mixing bowl. Put the bowl over the ice bath and stir frequently. Cool the cream to 140 degrees F (60 degrees C).

Remove the cream from the ice bath, cover the bowl tightly with plastic wrap, and put it in the refrigerator.

Use the same chocolate icing as in Recipe 1, and sprinkle chopped pistachios on top.

RECIPE 3: SALTED CARAMEL ÉCLAIRS

Makes 9

Ingredients:

- Choux shells

For Salted Caramel Pastry Cream:

- 1/2 cup sugar + 1/4 cup sugar
- 1/4 cup water
- 2 cups whole milk
- 1/4 cup cornstarch
- 1 large egg
- 2 large egg yolks
- 2 tbsp butter
- 1 tsp vanilla extract

- 1/4 tsp fleur de sel or sea salt

Combine 1/2 cup of sugar and the water in a medium saucepan. Bring to a boil, brush down the sides of the pan with water, and boil for 8 to 10 minutes, or until caramelized. Slowly stir in the milk. Return the pan to low heat and stir until smooth. Increase the heat to medium and heat to a simmer.

In a medium bowl, whisk together the corn-starch and 1/4 cup sugar. Whisk in the egg and egg yolks. As you whisk, add the hot caramel mixture and transfer the mixture back to the saucepan. Cook while whisking constantly over medium heat for 2 to 3 minutes, or until it thickens and just comes to a boil. Strain through a fine mesh sieve into a bowl and stir in butter, vanilla, and salt.

Pipe cream into the choux shells.

Caramel Icing:
- 2 tbsp butter
- 3 cups icing sugar, sifted (also called confec-tioners' sugar, powdered sugar, or xxx sugar)
- 4 tbsp milk
- 1 1/2 tsp caramel essence (from specialty stores)

Melt butter in a saucepan over low heat. Add icing sugar, milk, and caramel essence and beat it over the heat until smooth over. Dip the top of each éclair in the icing and let it cool.

RECIPE 4: HAZELNUT MOCHA ÉCLAIRS

Makes 9

Ingredients:
- Choux shells
- Hazelnut Mocha Filling
- 1 tbsp boiling water
- 2 cups heavy whipping cream
- 1/4 cup icing sugar/confectioners' sugar
- 1/2 cup chopped hazelnuts, divided
- 1 tbsp instant coffee granules

Dissolve coffee granules in boiling water. Let cool. In a bowl, beat cream and sugar until stiff peaks form. Fold in coffee mixture and hazelnuts. Refrigerate.

The chocolate icing is the same as in Recipe 1.

RECIPE 5: SAVORY ÉCLAIRS WITH SALMON, CREAM CHEESE AND FRESH HERBS

Savory éclairs make great appetizers or snacks. Using the same choux shells, you can fill it with a variety of different ingredients.

For this recipe, you need:
- Choux shells
- 1 1/2 cups cream cheese
- Fresh dill, finely chopped
- Fresh parsley, finely chopped
- A few sprigs of green onions, finely chopped
- Some salt
- A few drops of lemon juice
- Salmon slices

Mix the cream cheese, sour cream, dill, parsley, and

green onion in a bowl. Season with some salt and a few drops of lemon juice. Spread between the shells. Add slices of salmon.

More Savory Recipes

Here are some other savory combinations to try:

• Spinach, Gruyere cheese (or the cheese of your choice), and onion

• Ground lamb seasoned with cumin, salt, pepper, tzatziki sauce, and chopped black olives

• Beet puree with sour cream and horseradish

• Roasted eggplant and tomato sauce

• Shrimp, mushrooms, and shredded cooked carrots

• Chicken salad

ABOUT THE AUTHOR

Harper Lin is a *USA TODAY* bestselling cozy mystery author. When she's not reading or writing mysteries, she loves going to yoga classes, hiking, and hanging out with her family and friends.

For a complete list of her books by series, visit her website.

www.HarperLin.com